# PILGRIMS

**The Arts Council**
An Chomhairle Ealaíon

First published in 1998 by
Marino Books
16 Hume Street Dublin 2
Tel: (01) 661 5299; Fax: (01) 661 8583;
e.mail: books@marino.ie

Trade enquiries to CMD Distribution
55A Spruce Avenue
Stillorgan Industrial Park Blackrock
County Dublin
Tel: (01) 294 2556; Fax: (01) 294 2564

© John Evans 1998

ISBN 1 86023 070 9

10 9 8 7 6 5 4 3 2 1

A CIP record for this title is available
from the British Library

Cover design by
Penhouse Design Group
Printed in Ireland by ColourBooks
Baldoyle Industrial Estate, Dublin 13

Published in the US and Canada by
the Irish American Book Company
6309 Monarch Park Place, Niwot
Colorado 80503
Tel: (303) 652-2710; (800) 452-7115
Fax: (303) 652-2689; (800) 401-9705

# PILGRIMS

## JOHN EVANS

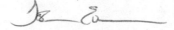

IRISH AMERICAN BOOK COMPANY (IABC)
Boulder, Colorado

*For Geraldine*

I

# WHO ART IN HEAVEN

I should be safe beside her, rest in peace. But I have tossed and turned through sleep tonight, a hand reaching for her now and then as, half awake, I search for reassurance. Her breathing speaks to me in semi-lucid moments, convincing me to sleep. Unwitting whisper. *It's okay, Michael, everything's okay.* And I become her baby, nestled against her, comforted to sleep.

I drift, castaway, unconscious. Fitful. My exhaustion makes it hard for me to slip beneath the surface, to roll deep with demersal disconnection. I am here, and not. Still running. Thoughts intrude, cerebral vapour trails, like snakes, sliding behind my eyelids. Jerk awake. Alert. Jolted into consciousness. Eyes snap open in darkness. Disoriented. Afterimages. Nightmare. Like a child. Stumbling, wild-eyed panic. Branches with faces, open-mouthed, screaming, call my name. Branches with hands, fingers pointing. *We know who you are.* Roots slither across my feet, winding around my ankles, pull me down, smother me. Back. I can't go back. There was a sound . . .

. . . 'Michael. The phone.'

'What? Fuck.' I pick it up. 'Hello?' I reach for the bedside lamp and snap it on. Christ. The light hurts my eyes. Blinding. I push the heel of my hand against my right eye socket. Stars. I can't see my watch. 'What time is it? Who is this?'

'Michael? Is that you?' My mother, voice straining down the line.

9

Maria stirs beside me. A small white arm edges its way from underneath the duvet, followed by a tousled, puzzled, blonde head. She squints at me through the brightness, mouthing questions. I turn my back to her, scowling.

'Jesus Christ, Mother, what is it? It's the middle of the night over here. What do you want?'

'Michael . . . Your father . . . I think you'd better come home . . . '

There are journeys that we don't anticipate and trips we hope we never have to make. Like children at a party game, we seek out hiding places. Illogical. Comfortable in mis-becoming discontent, we pray our compromises last forever. But everything decays. There are phone calls that we know will come in time, will wake us from our slumber, yet we sleep. And deep in sleep we need not justify. We hibernate and wait. Incogitant.

Dublin Airport was unusually quiet on Sunday morning. Subdued, as if for him. Frank Dunne, my father's oldest friend, was waiting. He was standing, cap in hand, like a late arrival at midnight Mass, neck craned, searching. Weak, wet eyes missed us as we wrestled our bags into the arrivals hall.

'Frank.' He jumped when I addressed him.

'Oh Jay. Michael. I didn't see you there.' He took my hand in both of his. The cold hands of an old man. Hard. Brittle. A wide smile climbed onto his face. 'How are you, hun? You're looking very well.' Then he became flustered, as if his momentary happiness was somehow inappropriate. His eyes fell away from mine, settling on his own scuffed shoes. His face grew grey and sombre, previous mischief missing from his eyes.

'Michael, I'm so sorry. He earned his place in heaven. He was a good man, you know. A saint if ever there was one.'

'Yeah, I know, Frank. One in a million.' I squeezed his

hand and then released it. 'Listen, it's good to see you, Frank. Thanks for coming. I don't think we could have faced the train. We're both knackered. Not much sleep last night. You remember Maria, don't you?'

He turned to her. 'Oh yes. Of course. It's nice to see you again, love.'

He nodded, hand extended. Maria smiled and took it. 'It's nice to see you too.'

'We'd better go,' he said to me. 'Your mammy will be waiting.'

Taking Maria's suitcase, he shepherded us towards the car park. It was raining outside. Some things never change. This June bore remarkable resemblance to all the others I could dredge up from my memory. I stood waiting while Frank paid for the car park, my face turned to the clouds, water settling in my hair. Maria held her coat above her head, watching me.

'It's strange,' I said. 'I thought it would feel different. Emptier or something.'

She smiled sadly, settled her coat around her shoulders, and touched my elbow. 'Life goes on, Michael.'

'For some of us.'

Frank waved a ticket from the doorway. 'Over here.'

We charged along the motorway, nudged our way through the bottleneck at Whitehall church, headed down the North Circular Road, and crossed the East-link toll-bridge. Frank fished frantically in his pockets for the requisite fifty-pence piece. *I know I have one somewhere.*

They left me alone with my thoughts for the entire journey to Wexford, tactfully leaving me out of their small-talk. Listening to the dull thwack of the windscreen wipers as they decapitated gathering beads of rain, I drifted through a private, melancholy eulogy.

*How did you get here, Michael? Remember him holding you when you were a child. The smell of his tobacco and the raw*

11

*scratch of his bristles when he kissed you goodnight. And now you are here to bury a stranger. How did you get here?*

There is a moment, like a cord snapping, when suddenly the bond between us shatters, leaving argument and awkwardness. The hero-worship ends. I realise, astonished, that he is not the biggest daddy on the street. Patriarch and pacifist, he would not beat up anyone for me. So Michael stands alone. Then school just peters out for me, like water running cold between numb fingers. One minute it surrounds me, filling every waking moment, the next it slips away, leaving me to mourn the passing of a childhood. Helpless, I watch my innocence betrayed. The best days of my life become anathema to me. I shed my infancy like dead skin and step across a threshold, wide-eyed. My graduation is a celebration. Preliminaries dispensed with, the main event is about to get under way. The world is my oyster and I am the pearl . . .

*How naive, how full of expectation.*

Perhaps I was an accident. A random copulation. It would explain a lot. Start as you mean to continue. The story of my life. A series of accidents waiting to happen. And I have been a worthy catalyst. I am an only child, conceived of only children. I told myself that roots were not important to people like me. This left me free to wander, stretch the leash, push the limits. A child of freedom with no emotional baggage to keep my feet on the ground, I was in control of my own destiny.

Inevitably, he rounded on me in a fit of rage. The context, the occasion, forgotten long ago. Just another argument. But I recall the spittle flying from the corners of his mouth, the fire in his eyes. As a man, I can almost feel his frustration, the trembling inside as he struggled to contain his disappointment in his son. 'Do you think the world revolves around you?' I returned his stare, dead-eyed and sullen, the air crackling between us, and maybe he saw dark thoughts, like storm clouds, drift behind my drooping eyelids. His world may not have, perhaps that is why we grew apart, but, Oh yes, most certainly. It was me at the centre of my universe. My world did revolve around me and everything I touched was a mere satellite, its purpose to keep me mused, to stave off boredom.

When I was eighteen I left home. I had grown tired of my parents. I ran away to Dublin and found a good job. Arrogant youth, I took it as a sign of greatness. My peers queued endlessly at the labour exchange in Anne Street for government money. All of them. In my mind, I was the only one to have made good. Of course, whenever I met old school colleagues, they would lie. I could see right through them. How dare they try to climb aboard my pedestal. There they were, floating in this great void, beseeching me to throw them a lifeline. I allowed them to bask in my presence, but refused to let them touch me.

Gradually I became lonely and sought out other deities: bankers, stockbrokers, insurance agents. We wore Armani suits and paisley ties and knew every barman in Dublin by name. I was happy for a while. But Ireland couldn't hold me. Nineteen-ninety-two beckoned and Europe opened its arms and begged me to become its lover. I gripped the bit between my teeth, kissed the Blarney stone goodbye, and vowed that I would never look back.

But I loved my father, even though we had not been close for a number of years. I believed he never quite forgave me for growing up and leaving him alone with my mother. Perhaps it was to spite him that I grew into a man who had little or nothing in common with him. He was selfless and easy-going, I was selfish and intense. We had many long debates, automatically opposing one another. To each his own, we would steadfastly refuse to budge an inch. Black to him was white to me. Never grey between us. Stubbornness shared. My inheritance.

The last time I saw him was in Dublin. I was there on business, reluctant. He met me at the Shelbourne Hotel for afternoon tea. I picked the Shelbourne on purpose, knowing that the air of affluence would make him feel uncomfortable. He despised falseness and loathed my yuppie tendencies. I revelled in his discomfort.

He came alone, asking my mother to give him this opportunity to talk with me *man to man*. His appearance shocked me, as it always did. There was ample time between my visits for age to tighten its grip on him. He seemed frail, the broad shoulders that carried me through my youth had been softened and rounded by time. He carried a cane, needing its support when he walked, but would not allow me to help him cross the foyer. I was embarrassed by him, thinking that every eye in the room must surely be tracing our slow, painful progress through the clutter and jumble of tables and chairs. He hobbled resolutely towards the farthest table he could find, eventually sighing and lowering his ancient body into the folds of an antique couch. We sat opposite each other, like chess players waging war.

'How's Mother?'

'Fine. She sends her best. Maria?'

'Very well.'

We listened to the careful sound of teacups rattling on saucers.

'The weather's nice.' I tried again.

'Yes. Thanks be to God.'

A waitress came and stood by his elbow, pen poised.

'Tea for two,' I said. 'And sandwiches. What would you like, Dad? Cheese or ham?'

He looked around slowly, taking stock of the room. 'Cucumber seems the obvious choice. I take it we'll be having strawberries and cream for dessert.' He smiled sweetly at the scribbling waitress. 'My son has expensive tastes.'

Round one to my father.

Ordering over, we tried to make polite conversation, but I knew that something was bothering him. He looked distracted, drifting off midway through sentences, fondling the handle of his cane and staring into space.

'What's wrong, Dad? You look worried. Do you need money?'

Something flickered across his face for a moment. He looked as if he was about to say something, then changed his mind and swallowed, gulping back his anger. He stared past my shoulder, searching for the best way to broach the subject. At last he looked at me. Direct. Straight. Both feet first.

'Your mother is not a happy woman, Michael. She's afraid of being alone. You know. When I'm gone.'

'Oh Jesus.'

He touched his chest, bowing his head almost imperceptibly at my profanity.

'Michael. It's time you made your peace.'

'There's no peace to make, Dad. Nothing's wrong.' I smiled across the table at him, shaking my head. He stared at me. Waiting. I sighed and ran a hand through my hair, my eyes dropping away from his, focusing on his tie-pin, the one I gave him for his birthday. 'Look, Dad,' I said slowly, as if speaking to a child, 'we've been through all this before. I keep telling you there is no problem. It's normal. I live in Germany. That's why we don't see that much of each other. Flights cost a fortune, you know.'

'Michael . . . '

'I'll see her at Christmas. Okay?'

He folded his hands across his cane, his mouth set in a hard, determined line. He clicked his tongue, thinking, before he spoke. 'Say what you will, Michael, but I'm not stupid and I'm not getting any younger. I know how the two of you fight like cats and dogs behind my back and I want you to sort it out once and for all. Will you do that for me? Set my mind at ease?'

He was leaning towards me, all serious eyes and earnest expression, determined. He was not going to let me get away too easily this time. I opened my mouth, ready to sidestep. *Sure, sure. Anything you say.* But suddenly I felt an anger grow in me, emotion surging to the surface, like a diver, out of oxygen. *Fuck this. No. I will not be dragged back. I have escaped already.* But Ireland was trying to get on level terms with me again. *Not so fast. Get back, you bollox.*

'Let's nip this in the bud, Dad. Okay? I'm not in the humour for another one of your sermons.' My voice was surprisingly even. I had learned to hide my emotions from him. 'This is just another guilt trip.'

'Michael, I . . . '

'We have a little problem here. Don't we?'

He looked at me, his lips pressed together, swallowing. His Adam's apple bobbed against the loose neck of his shirt. He hadn't shaved properly. Tufts of hair congregated underneath his chin.

'It seems we do.' He spoke softly, his disappointment tangible.

'Well I'll tell you what the problem is, shall I? What you don't understand, what my mother doesn't understand, is that there's a great big world out there. And I live in it. Now, here's the thing. To me Ireland is just a little shit-hole. A dive. And every Paddy seems to think that it's some sort of Mecca that he has to work his arse off to get back to some day. Well, not this Paddy. I'm not coming back. I'm gone for good.'

'I see.'

'Do you? Good. You see, my life isn't here any more. I have no ties here except you two. I know well what my mother wants. She wants me to settle down here and sire lots of grandchildren for her to babysit on Saturday nights. Well that's the last thing in the world that I want, so it's not going to happen.'

'Michael, no one is . . . '

'I like my life as it is, Dad. Sin and all. You're just going

16

to have to get used to the fact that I'm not going to get married for my mother's sake. I'm sorry and all. I know that you're ashamed. But I won't be preached to just because the nosey old bitches loitering outside Sunday Mass have nothing better to do than damn my soul to hell.'

'Michael. Stop. Enough.' He held a withered finger in front of my face, an effort at authority. 'I don't know how this started. I didn't come here to fight with you. This is not about you living with Maria. What you do, how you live your life, is your business. Just don't ask me to endorse your behaviour. You know what I think.'

'What you're told to think,' I spat. 'Well as far as I'm concerned, the Catholic Church can shag off. There's more to life than marriage, children and pretending contraception doesn't exist.'

The tea and sandwiches arrived. We paused awkwardly as the waitress settled the contents of a large brown tray in front of us. He thanked her warmly, I remained aloof. I watched her walk away, the shape of her embossed against her uniform.

He leaned towards me again, sighing. 'Son,' attempting to appease me, 'I know you have your own life, and I know you think you know what's best. I'm not going to argue with you. You're old enough and ugly enough to make your own mistakes. Okay?' He smiled and hesitated for a moment. 'All I'm asking is that you let your mother know that you'll be there for her if she needs you. Being old can be very lonely, Michael. You are the only flesh and blood we have. You owe it . . . '

'I repaid my debt years ago,' I snapped, frustrated. I could negotiate million- pound business deals with men twice my age, but when it came to my father I was eight years old. 'I owe you nothing.'

He sat back against his cushions and regarded me, his petulant child, his eyes narrow. 'Is that what we are to you? A debt? Do you think you have to pay us back for something?

17

Well, debt paid in full, sunshine. You're right. You owe us nothing. I don't want anything from you. I was going to say you owe it to yourself. Here it is, Michael.' He leaned forward, almost whispering. 'Maybe for your own sake you should think about your mother. Think of it as an opportunity. Life is too short for this sort of shite, Michael. Say the things you want to say now, while you still have the chance. I'm old, Michael. I know things. It goes with the territory.'

He stopped then, our faces inches apart, his blue eyes locked to mine. Like mine. *He has your eyes.* I blinked twice and looked away.

'Okay, Dad. I'm sorry. I'll sort it out. Okay?' I could not see the point in continuing this argument with him. 'Listen. The tea is going cold.'

We ate our sandwiches and drank our tea, avoiding any further contentious issues, both realising that it was pointless to try to resolve our differences.

I shared a taxi with him to Connolly Station. As I watched him shuffle away down the platform, I suddenly remembered him as he was when I was a child, walking down the road on a sunny summer's day, his suit jacket flung over his shoulder, a broad smile on his face. I remembered him vaulting the fence, running to where I sat playing on the grass, lifting me and flinging me, laughing, in the air, like a rag-doll. I wanted to follow him to the train, to tell him that of course I would look after my mother when he was gone, that he could depend on me, that he did not have to worry about a thing. I watched him share a joke with a young couple who were helping him to board the train. He turned on the top step and waved at me. I should have followed him. I should have hugged him and kissed him and thanked him for being the wonderful man that he was. I didn't. I raised my hand and slowly waved back. The door closed, a whistle blew, and I lost the chance forever.

We rounded a corner and entered the last village before Wexford town. I recalled my father's old tradition, returning from our many trips to *the big smoke*. 'Where are we now?' he would roar over his shoulder as he navigated this selfsame bend. I, as a four, six, eight or eighteen-year-old, would shout back 'Castlebridge'. My mouth smiled at Maria. My eyebrows climbed my forehead.

'Where are we now?' I whispered.

'Huh?'

Three and a half miles later we crossed Wexford Bridge, the scene of the pilgrimage within the pilgrimage, where I had sneered so often, from the comfort of my father's car, at a forest of thumbs, each one beseeching us to bear its owner to the Unyoke Inn in search of passion, pleasure and pints. Rain, hail or snow, there they would be, every Saturday night. Prodigal children, trekking from all over to participate in this most sacred of traditions. I attended on one occasion, sick from drink, a gate-crashed twenty-first . . .

. . . The earth did not move.

The house is in Coolcotts. Unassuming. Three bedrooms, a small garden in the front. 'There you are, Michael. Home.' Frank spun the wheel, the car curving across the driveway, and dropped us at the doorstep. Delivery.

Home. It wasn't mine. Not any more. I had made it clear years before, no point maintaining the shrine that was once my room. I wouldn't live there again. My mother documented my decision by placing a large *B&B* sign at the front gate. She put strangers in my bed, where, pubescent, wet-dream waking, I had clutched myself, embarrassed, sperm spilling into the sheets. My father's sacred inner sanctum, the spare room, where, like a giant magpie, he gathered everything he could lay his hands on, had also been violated to make way for paying customers.

He lived here for all his married life. Carried her across the threshold, maybe. Her, laughing, dressed in white, her

19

bouquet dangling down his back. He whispered that he loved her in the hall. *We're home. Our home.* She felt his arms under her, and kissed him on the lips. *I want to have your children. I'm so happy* . . . Or maybe they arrived, exhausted, and stood there with their shoes in hand, looking at the stairs. *Too early to go to bed, I think.* She nodded, nervous too . . .

She heard the engine and came rushing to the doorway, dressed in black. I felt like Norman. Manic. *Mother. I'm home.*

'Michael.'

'Mother.'

Wary, we wound around each other, like two cocks before a fight. I wanted to say something nice. To reach for her. But she stood with her hands clasped in front of her, shoulders set. Her face was a mask to me. I saw no opening. Perhaps I didn't look very hard.

'How are you holding up?'

'Okay. Under the circumstances.' Her voice sounded slightly ragged, as if she had been crying. 'Come inside.'

'Let me get the bags.'

I turned to see Maria and Frank standing side-by-side behind the car. They had piled the bags beside them and were watching us, confused, expecting something more.

'Let's go inside.'

'I really should be going,' said Frank.

'Ah Frank,' my mother said, 'come in and have some tea.'

He looked at me, hesitating. I looked back at him, not realising. I had become the man of the house. He shifted his attention back to her, glancing back and forth between us. 'No, Kate. I really have to go.'

'Thanks for the lift, Frank.' Maria took his arm, smiling. 'It was so good of you.'

'Not at all. The least I could do.' He looked self-conscious, standing beside her in his raincoat and cloth cap. I felt a smile touch my lips. Somehow distant from the scene, I was a spectator. Removed.

'Michael?' Maria was staring at me.

20

'What? Oh. Yeah. Listen, thanks, Frank. For everything. We'll see you no doubt.' I held out a hand.

'Goodbye, Michael.' He shook hands formally, taking his cap off first. 'Again, my heartfelt condolences.'

'Thanks, Frank. I appreciate it. I really do.'

He stepped back, replacing his cap, and cleared his throat. 'Goodbye, Kate. And if there's anything I can . . . You know . . . ' Leaving his sentence trailing, he climbed back into his car and left us alone to mourn our dead.

The living-room had not changed significantly since I was a child. An antique dresser, solid oak, stood proudly in the corner, displaying my grandmother's best china. The carpet had grown a little more threadbare, patches of exposed concrete peeking out from under throw-down rugs. The old beige couch engulfed and embraced me like a long lost friend.

My mother opened the whiskey I had bought at Frankfurt Airport. She poured three small measures, handing one to each of us. I sipped my drink and stared into the fire. A fire. In June. It was thirty-two degrees in Frankfurt. February here.

'I wish he had listened.' She swirled the drink in the bottom of her glass, untouched. 'I told him to give up those bloody cigarettes. He was an awful man. Couldn't be told.'

'He was seventy years old, mother.' She looked at me, as if realising for the first time that I was there. 'There's no point in thinking about cigarettes and things. When it's time, it's time. Giving up smoking wouldn't have made much difference.' I drained my drink and held the glass out to her. 'Can I have another?'

'Help yourself.' She walked past me and sat on a stool beside the dresser, her drink held in her lap, thumb rubbing absent-mindedly along the rim of the glass. I remembered birds, when I was a child, swooping hard against the window, crumbling, and lying stunned on the grass outside. She would retrieve them, gentle, and sit like that, stroking, whispering to them, until their heartbeats had returned to normal. *Do you want to touch him, Michael?* I am four, maybe. Frightened, faltering, I extend a hand, feeling feathers soft against my fingertips, like felt. *Can you feel his heart?* Together we release it. Her opening her hands, an offering. Wings spread wide against the sky, it flutters from her. Or sometimes we would find them, necks broken, flightless in the flowerbeds. Funerals. She would stand beside me at the grave, holding my small hand in hers. Shoe-boxes are dotted around her garden, like mines. I remembered this. Our secret. Now it was my turn to hold her hand beside a grave.

She looked up, eyes shining, tears starting to force their way to the surface. 'I can't believe he's gone.'

The strength had been an act. For me. It had been so long since we had shown tenderness to each other that she had been afraid to reveal her true feelings, not knowing how I would react. My heart felt heavy in my chest and I had to blink back my own tears. I stood up, crossed the room, and knelt in front of her, taking her hands in mine. Maria coughed, excused herself, and went to the kitchen to put the kettle on.

'Mammy.' I hadn't called her that in years. 'It's going to be all right. I'm here now. We'll get through this together.'

She sniffed, looking away from me and biting at her lower lip. 'You're here now, but tomorrow or the next day you'll be gone back to Germany with her.' She pointed towards the kitchen with her chin. Maria. 'What will I do then? I'm sixty-five years old, Michael. I don't want to be alone.'

I put a hand on her cheek and pulled her face around, gently, until she was looking into my eyes. She sniffed again, rubbing at her nose. 'Mammy,' I said, as softly as I could. 'Listen to me now. You're going to be all right. We're all going to be all right. You *will* survive.'

Her shoulders started to rock. She gave up all pretence of control. Tears started streaming down her face. I rubbed her cheek with my thumb, my own tears coming now, mirroring hers. 'Oh, Michael. Why did he have to leave me?'

I stood, knees cracking, and put my arms around her. 'I don't know, Mammy,' I said, holding her head against my stomach. 'I honestly don't know.'

'What am I going to do, Michael?'

'We'll think of something.'

It was all that I could think of to say.


It rained all day on Tuesday. My father had been a popular man. We stood under a black umbrella by the graveside for an eternity, shaking hands, listening to murmured words of condolence, and looking brave. Father Cullen, the parish priest, told us that he knew for a fact that my father was in heaven and that, one day, we would all be reunited in the glory of God. My mother thanked him for his words, I glowered and bit my tongue.

'Well, Michael,' he said, 'how are things in Germany? Are ye going to give us a day out soon?' He looked meaningfully at Maria.

'Thanks all the same, but I think one family occasion per year is enough.' I stared straight into his eyes, smiled coldly, and waited for him to look away. It was my prerogative, my father was the one in the coffin. He coughed, excusing himself, anxious to be gone.

'You should drop by for confession before you go back, Michael. Sure it must be hard enough to find an understanding priest off in Germany. Eh?'

'Fucking clergy,' I snarled to Maria as he moved away through the crowd, bestowing the odd smile or *bless you* on fawning parishioners. 'Understanding me bollox.'

'Michael, be good, will you?' she said. 'For your mother's sake. Don't be a prick all your life.'


It seemed as though we played host to most of Wexford that evening, my mother providing an endless supply of tea

23

and sandwiches. Mourners gathered in groups in the living-room, balancing cups and saucers in their hands, like jugglers. Red-faced laughter echoed round the walls. She moved amongst them, filling cups with tea and hands with food. They were immune to her, unconscious of the effort she was making. Everyone but Frank. He stood apart, silent. We were bookends, scowling at the crowd. I laced my tea with whiskey and wished that I was anywhere but there, sur-rounded by well-wishers and professional funeral attenders.

Every now and then a grey head would appear before me, springing into place like a withered jack-in-the-box. *I was your daddy's friend. We went way back. The last time I saw you, you were a little boy.* Some looked familiar, shrunken parodies of people I once knew.

'You okay?' asked Maria, passing with plates of canapés.

I shook my head. 'It's like a fucking senile circus here. I think I'm going mad.'

'Patience, Michael,' she whispered, leaning over to kiss my cheek. 'It'll be over soon.'

A few minutes later Frank put a hand on my shoulder. 'Maria says you're going a bit stir crazy.'

I smiled. 'You could say that.'

'Fancy a little walk?'

'Frank, I thought you'd never ask.' He smiled and took my arm, leading me towards the front door.

We stood beneath an oak tree in the garden, a comfortable silence between us. Frank smoked a cigarette. Soft rain still fell, big drops bouncing on the canopy of leaves above our heads.

'I think it's down for the day,' said Frank, looking at the sky, black clouds looming ominously close.

'Yeah. Looks that way.'

'Aye.' He blew smoke through his nostrils, studying the end of his cigarette. His nose was bulbous and red, broken blood vessels criss-crossing just beneath the skin. He dropped the cigarette on the grass and stubbed it out with his toe.

Black shoes. Black suit. Like an undertaker. He looked at me, final wisps of smoke escaping from the corners of his mouth. 'Are you okay, Michael?'

I smiled. 'Yeah, Frank. Thanks for asking. Or at least I will be.'

'I meant what I said, you know. If there's anything I can do. I knew your daddy for a long time. We went to school together. That wasn't today nor yesterday.'

'No. I suppose not.'

We stood again, awkward now, something left unsaid.

'Michael?' He was standing close to the tree, old fingers picking at the bark. 'It's probably none of my business, but . . . Well, what about your mother?'

'What about her, Frank?'

'It's just that . . . You know . . . Your daddy . . . ' He sighed and tried again. 'Who's going to look after her?'

He stood still then, studying me, his hand lying flat against the tree trunk, eyes steady, locked on mine. I pulling at my ear lobe. 'Well, Frank, I meant to talk to you about that. I was hoping you might keep an eye on her for me. While I'm not here. You know?'

He nodded solemnly, an acolyte, eager for instruction. 'Of course, Michael. Sure. Anything.'

'Thanks, Frank,' I said, patting his shoulder. 'I knew I could count on you.'

He called me as I walked across the lawn towards the front door. 'Michael?'

I turned back to him, rain rattling in the undergrowth around me. 'Yeah, Frank?'

'It would be my pleasure, you know. Kate is very special. I've always thought . . . You know . . . That she was special.'

I looked at him, his grey hair slicked against his head. His nicotine-stained fingers were locked together in front of him, as if in prayer. He was leaning towards me, almost expectant. Waiting for my blessing, perhaps. *Randy old fucker.*

'That she is, Frank,' I said. 'Special. Come on in now. We're getting soaked.'

The last of the hangers-on drifted away at about midnight. My mother looked exhausted. Ignoring her protests, Maria managed to get her to go to bed, leaving us with the cleaning up. I kissed her goodnight and watched her wearily climb the stairs. Maria came over and put her arms around me.

'How are you bearing up?' she asked. 'Are you all right?'

'Yeah, sure. You know me, I've got no heart. Jaysus, I just wish this was all over and I could get away from this shit-hole. I fucking hate Ireland.'

'No you don't. You just think you do.' She kissed me on the lips, tightening her arms around me, tender squeeze.

'Come on then,' she said. 'Let's get this mess cleared up.'

*A child running on a beach. Dipping in and out of waves, one hand held above his head. Exuberant exultation. Blood pumps through veins, the heart applauds. Sun beating, gulls crying, sand hot beneath bare feet. Sheer joy. Alive . . .*

*. . . Lost. I am a man. Trudging, puffing along the strand. Legs aching, chest heaving. My heart protests. I do this because I must. Cardiovascular commitments. I have to watch what I eat now. No more sticky buns for Michael.*

*The funeral is over. Life is no longer what it used to be. We must accept this, we must do what is necessary. What is necessary? Must I take responsibility for the redintegration of my childhood could-have-beens? No, they are lost. As surely as the child's innocent acceptance of the perfect body time has not yet raped and mutilated. All that is left to me is this tinge of regret, this ocean of apprehension and, I fear, no choice but to continue along this path which fate has preordained. To change would require courage. Courage I do not have.*

I run on, ignoring the pain in my side. Each step takes me closer to confrontation. A conversation I don't want to have. But I know I have to face her. Sweat soaks through my jogging suit, the wind whips my hair against my face. I can see Culleton's Gap now, wooden steps leading into the dunes. My mother is waiting in the car. She insisted on accompanying me. *It will do me good to get out of the house. I've always liked a nice drive.* Soon now. Panting, I stop, my hands on my knees, and squint out at the ocean, back bent, bile bitter in my throat. I spit on the sand, saliva swinging from my mouth, wiped away with the back of my hand. A car ferry inches its way towards Rosslare Harbour. Seagulls swoop and soar noisily above the surf, some struggling against the wind. A gaggle of children squeal and splash a little further down the shore. I feel a combination of responsibility and helplessness mixed with an overwhelming desire to get as far away from here as possible.

Gradually my breathing becomes regular. I am ready now.

Almost. I did not want to face her in a weakened state. I will need my strength. Straightening, my hands pushed against the small of my back, I breathe the sea air. Landlocked in Germany has its disadvantages. *God. I miss the sea.*

When I get to the car she is staring out the window. Drifting, she does not appear to notice me approaching. The door, opening, startles her, chasing her from whichever corner she has chosen as her hiding place. I can tell she has been crying. Her eyes are red and puffy. Sitting heavily into the driver's seat, only slightly out of breath now, my composure regained, I put a hand on hers where they lie folded in her lap. A crumpled tissue is wrapped around her fingers. She smiles at me, freeing a hand to dab away the last of her tears. They are private. Not to be shared with me.

'You okay, Mother?' Wiping sweat from my forehead.

She nods. 'Do you put yourself through that every day?'

'It's your fault, Mother. Too many desserts when I was a child.'

We sit in silence for a moment, each of us locked in our own peculiar melancholy, smiles on our lips, pain in our hearts. Distant memories reveal hopes and opportunities, now gone and lost forever.

I break the silence, sighing. 'We can't put it off forever, can we?'

'What?'

'What plans have you got?'

Her smile fades, worried wrinkles running slowly down her face. Her eyes drift from mine, unfocused. 'Oh. None, I suppose. I never thought . . . ' Her words dribble into nothingness, swallowed by the grief she feels for him.

'Don't worry, Mother. It's okay.' I squeeze her hand. 'We just need to think about it. That's all.'

She smiles again, nervous. 'Does it have to be now?'

'Yeah. I think it does.'

'Oh, Michael. I knew it was coming, of course. It's hard to really face up to these things, though. I mean, to think about it while he was still alive. I couldn't.'

28

'I know, Mother. We have to face it now though. We have to get you sorted out.'

'Your father and I were never ones for planning ahead.' It is as if she hasn't heard me. 'You were always good for planning. When you were a little boy even. Saving your pocket money for something or other. You always had a plan. I don't know where you got that from.' Suddenly she looks at me, returning. 'I don't know what I'm going to do, Michael. But don't you worry. I'll think of something.'

'Oh sweet Jesus, Mother.' I withdraw my hand from hers and run it through my hair, frustrated. 'How many Irish mammies does it take to change a light bulb?'

'What?' Her brow furrows.

'None, I'll just sit here in the dark while you go out and enjoy yourself, son.' She looks at me as if I have gone mad. 'You're being ridiculous, Mother. Of course I'm going to worry.'

She turns away from me, her back stiffening, clutching her handbag in her lap. In profile, I can see her jaw setting, her lips pursed as if she is biting back her words. 'Michael, it's not your problem. I'm well able to look after myself.'

'That's not the point, for Christ's sake.' I realise that I have spoken more sharply than I had intended to. I try to soften my tone, 'Look, Mother . . . ' Softer, almost whisper. 'Mammy . . . I'm just trying to find out what I can do to help you. You have to make some big decisions, you know. If you can't talk to me, who can you talk to? I want to help. Okay?'

'Okay.' Her voice has softened too. She is trying not to fight with me. 'I'm sorry. I'm very tired, Michael.' When she turns back to me there is a weariness in her that frightens me. A submission of sorts. 'I don't know what I'm going to do. I honestly don't. I'm not really able to think straight right now though, Michael. Decisions will have to wait.' She catches my hand again, firmly this time, as if trying to squeeze some sense into it. 'Everything will be all right. Stop worrying,

29

will you? You'll give yourself an ulcer. Like I said, it's not your problem.'

'You keep saying that,' I snap at her, beginning to lose my temper. 'Of course it's my problem. Who the hell else have you got? Frank? Jesus. Talk about the blind leading the blind.'

'Michael.' Her voice is hard, a warning. 'I'm really not able for this now. Don't push me.'

It is enough to stop me. 'I'm sorry. I didn't mean . . .' I bite my lip, afraid that I will cry. 'It's just . . . Everyone is so concerned about you. You know? You're not the only one who's grieving.' I am not proud of myself. She is fragile, vulnerable, and I can only think about myself. *Don't kick her when she's down, Michael. Stomp all over her instead.*

'I've been worrying about you, Michael,' she tells me, tenderly. 'And Maria. We've both been trying to support you.' My anger sputters, fizzles out. I feel ashamed for adding to her burden. 'He missed you when you left, you know.' She leans towards me, putting a hand on my cheek and turning my face to hers. 'He was so proud. He used to tell perfect strangers about his son with the big job in Germany.'

I smile sadly. 'I can imagine.'

'He loved you very much.'

I bite my lip, feeling tears threaten again. 'Oh Jesus.' I untangle myself from her, gripping the steering wheel with both hands. 'This isn't helping anyone.'

'It's good to talk about it, Michael. Tell me what you're feeling.'

*. . . What I'm feeling? How can she possibly understand what I am feeling? I had been secure in the knowledge that my father would be there if I needed him. A safety net to catch me if I fell. Now, I recall a story I have heard about a father who stands his toddler son on a table. 'Jump off,' he says. 'I'll catch you. Come on, trust me, son.' The child jumps and the father watches him crash to the floor. 'Let that be a lesson to you,' he says to his bleeding son. 'Never trust anyone.' I am that toddler now,*

30

*teetering on the brink, knowing that my father will never be there to catch me again. How could she understand that feeling? The painful realisation. Something so basic, at the very core of me, snatched away. No time left . . .*

'I don't know what to feel.' *They are not for you, Mother, not these feelings. Telling you would expose me.*

'I know what you mean, Michael. One minute I'm completely numb, the next I'm just overcome with despair. I don't know what I'm going to do, Michael.'

The moment of truth. 'You could always come back to Germany with us.' I don't look at her. Instead, I sit holding the steering wheel, staring out the window.

'Thanks, but no thanks, Michael. My life is here, not in someone else's home.'

'Maria? You don't like her much, do you?' I can feel the anger swell in me again. 'You know damn well you'd be welcome.'

'No I wouldn't. And we both know that Maria is not the problem.'

There is an awkward silence. She knows. I cannot hide it. Maria is an excuse. I have spent my whole life trying to escape my roots and now I am terrified that they will stretch out, claw at my heels, and drag me back where I came from.

'I can't come back.' The words come clipped, like bullets aimed at her.

'Nobody asked you.' Venom in her voice.

Hostility, controlled before, is loose now. A gesture made, half-hearted, brings old feelings to the surface. My father's death cannot repair the damage we have done to one another, pushing and pummelling for years. Now, when we need each other most, I realise that my mother and I are strangers. An odd success. Estranged, we are like tumbling trapeze artists, stretching, barely out of reach. A chasm awaits.

She has become a millstone, my responsibility. I am all this woman has, her last surviving relative. Who else will see her through old age? I cannot walk away from this. Lost

31

in a tunnel, I cannot see light at either end. She frightens me. She is not part of my plan. This does not fit the master scheme. She is a parameter that I have missed, a gremlin in the system. Here I am, sitting in a parked car, looking at the sand-dunes and searching for some way out. I think of all the other rocks and hard places I have wriggled from between, and all the people I have walked on in the process. *This is my mother, for Christ's sake. My flesh and blood. I can't just leave her here. Alone. Can I?* My last shred of decency recoils from this betrayal. I loathe my weakness, my selfishness. Is this me? Is this what all this struggle and pain has led to? I sigh, fighting down the genealogical claustrophobia which threatens to engulf me.

'You're right,' I say. 'This isn't the time to talk about this, is it?'

Her face softens. I can see tears, struggling to the surface again. 'No. It's all a bit raw still.' She smiles at me and touches my face. 'Let's go home, Michael.'

The next few days were a blur, the telephone driving us all mad, constantly ringing. Jangling, like nerve endings. Well-wishers asked insipid questions and made mundane comments. *A happy release.* Happy for whom? Do I sound ecstatic?

'Michael,' said Maria. 'For God's sake. Be nice. They mean well.'

'Fuckers.'

'Don't be rude.'

She was not impressed by my behaviour, but she bit her tongue and made allowances. She would touch my arm from time to time, or smile, or hug me when my mother left the room, coming to perch on the arm of my chair. My father's chair. My coldness baffled her, the way my eyes would slide away from contact. Greased things, hard to hold.

In bed she would whisper, holding me, having found me under cover of the darkness.

'Are you okay?'

32

'Yeah.'

'Michael. Talk to me.'

'Not now. I need to go to sleep.'

And in the morning she'd be gone. In deference to my mother. Appropriate, as always. Her perfume lingered, like the memory of her, warm against my back, arms around me, kissing my shoulder as I drifted into dreams. At breakfast she would smile across the coffee pot, pouring, and I would look away, studying a bottle on a shelf.

I avoided my mother. We passed each other in corridors, like oil-tankers in fog, cautiously aware of one another. It was Maria who held us together, a common thread. Umbilical. No love lost between them, but my mother seemed to cling to her those first few painful days. They cooked and cleaned together, finding comfort in the commonplace. My mother must have spoken of her loss. Maria listened while I sulked in far-flung corners of the house, looking at his ties. Or finishing a jigsaw puzzle, shattered when he died. *Ah Dad, you got that wrong. That's not an eye.*

We ate our meals in silence, breaking bread together. Chewing in unison. *Pass the salt please. Thanks.* Maria made efforts to unite us, throwing morsels on the table. *Frank said he'd come to cut the lawn tomorrow.* Potential conversations trickled past, awkward. Swallowed with sips of wine or lost with lifted coffee cups. And in the kitchen, later, she would hiss at me. *Michael, you could try to make an effort.* I would shrug, plunging my hands into soapy water, ignoring her wringing the tea towel in frustration. Meanwhile, my mother would answer the telephone in the other room. *Fuckers.*

*Sometimes a name escapes me. A face swims into view, spectre. Standing in Grafton Street, I am accosted. Confronted by the past. Classmate.*

'Michael Dwyer. How the hell are you?'

*And I am lost. Speechless, I stare. Baffled. I know you. Reflex responses, like words in a church. Chanted. Automatic. Meaningless. We talk.*

*'Remember Paul Dunne?' he says. I don't. 'He's doing really well now. Big in advertising.'*

*Time for introduction passes, stumbling away in awkward silence. Maria waits, eyes wide, wondering. She lets go of my hand. Disgusted. I am smiling, nodding, asking inane questions.*

*'Look, it was nice to see you,' he says, 'I've got to run. I have to meet the wife. I've got two kids now, you know. If you're home at Christmas give us a bell.'*

*He is gone. Back into my acne-ridden youth. She is looking at me, eyebrows raised, waiting for an explanation. I stare back, indignant, stubborn.*

*'That was very rude,' she states, folding her arms.*

*It annoys me, this fickle memory of mine. Torturing me with trivia. A face in a film. What have I seen him in before? A word. Missing. Betrayed, I flounder in front of friends, suddenly mute. A school-friend's name. Lost.*

*'I couldn't remember his name,' I say, darkly. 'I just couldn't remember his fucking name.'*

*Days later it will surface. Lying beside her in bed, I will turn to her, smiling. She will look at me, quizzical, 'What?' written on her face. My smile will widen and I will produce this gem with the practised flourish of a capable conjurer.*

*'Graham Kielty.'*

*A shattered past falls perfectly together.*

The Crow's Nest was . . . the Crow's Nest. The crowd slightly older, but the same crowd. Faces were familiar, people I had chosen not to know. They laughed, they drank, they flirted, they lived. I passed among them as a ghost. Ethereal, anonymous. They did not note my passing, nor my father's. I fancy that I lingered here and there, unnoticed. A snatched phrase, a word, a jumbled conversation. I leaned against the bar. The barman was somebody's little brother.

'A pint of Guinness, please.'

He nodded and shuffled sideways, like a crab, gathering a glass along the way.

When my pint arrived I sipped it and looked around, afraid that I might recognise someone. More afraid that I would not. A tap on my shoulder. *Sorry to hear about your da.* Muttered. I did not know him. He did not meet my eye. Then he was gone, fading back into the crowd. *Thanks.* Too late.

Paddy Murtagh appeared at my side. 'Well, Master Dwyer, as I live and breathe.'

*Ferret. I hated you at school. You're still trying to grow that moustache, I see. Your mannerisms are just like your old man's used to be. What are you, thirtysomething going on seventy-nine. Cock-of-the-walk now, aren't you? Biggest fish in the pond. Well it's a very fucking small pond and all us other fish got out.* 'How are ya, Paddy?'

'Nobody calls me that any more. My name is Patrick.'

*Bollox. Once a Paddy, always a Paddy.* 'Okay. How are you, Patrick?'

'Fine. Fine. Where are you now?'

*Standing two feet in front of you, you fucking moron.* 'Germany. What are you up to these days?'

'The same, the same.' . . . *Which is? . . .* 'Give us a call the next time you're home. We must get together and chat about the good old days.'

*I'll be sure to phone ahead and make an appointment. Prick. I used to beat you up.* 'Yeah, I'll look forward to it. See you, Paddy.'

'Patrick.'

'Right. Patrick. See you, Paddy.'

He slid off down the bar and stood on his own, clutching a pint glass almost as big as himself. Poor pathetic bastard. I almost felt sorry for him.

I finished my drink and ordered another. While I waited, I found a payphone in the corridor and phoned Claire. I had looked up her number the morning of the funeral, but couldn't think of what to say. It had been five years. *Hi Claire, it's Michael. My father's dead.*

'Hello.'

'Is Claire there?'

'Speaking.'

'Hi. It's Michael.'

'Sorry?'

'Michael Dwyer.'

Stunned silence.

'Michael? Jesus. How are you?' She shouts into the phone, amazed to hear from me, then catches herself, remembering. 'I just heard about your dad. I'm so sorry.'

'Yeah . . . Thanks . . . Eh . . . Listen. How would you like to buy an old mate a drink?'

'What? Now?' Incredulous.

'Why not? I'm in the Crow's Nest.'

She hadn't changed. Perhaps I didn't want her to have. She looked straight at me the minute she walked in the door, broke into that funny grin of hers and seemed to float across the floor. We embraced. Was it my imagination? Did she hold me a fraction longer than necessary? She held my hands, leaning back to look up into my face.

'Look at you. You look great. Jesus, I can't believe it. A phone call out of the blue after all this time.' She was still smiling. 'Why didn't you answer my letters, you bastard?'

I tried to look cute and helpless. 'Sorry?'

'You should be.' Mock annoyance. 'Frankly, I'm amazed I'm talking to you at all.' She broke into a smile again. 'Now give me another hug, you big oaf.'

We hugged again. This time she kissed my neck and squeezed so hard that I thought if she didn't hurt me, she would hurt herself.

'I take it yours is still a G&T,' I said. 'I took the liberty.'

'It is. I'm impressed. But how did you know I'd come? I only said maybe.'

36

'I had a good feeling. Besides, it's a small price to pay to impress the infamous Claire Roche.'

I had found a reasonably quiet table by the wall. There we were. Old friends, old stomping ground. Old feelings? I watched her as she talked. Her mouth. A suggestion of lipstick. For me? Her ear. A simple gold ringlet dangling from her perfect, perforated lobe. A dark wisp of hair casually touched away.

'Remember how I used to con you out of your chocolate in primary school?' Her eyes were alive with mischief.

I smiled. 'A fool and his chocolate are easily parted. How did you manage that?'

'I used to threaten to tell everybody that you kissed me behind the bicycle shed.'

'Did I?' I raised an eyebrow, looking at her steadily.

She laughed. 'Not when we were in primary school.'

'Oh?'

'I think we may have gone there after my debs.'

'You think?'

'Okay. You took me there after my debs.'

I ran a finger around the rim of my pint glass. 'Jesus. I thought I was a bit more romantic than that. I must have been pretty pissed.'

'You could say that. When I say you took me, it would probably be more accurate to say we carried each other. I think the only one more drunk than you that night was me. Your fault, I believe. Although I can't really blame you. You did warn me that you were trying to get me drunk and take advantage.'

I smiled at her. 'Now that you mention it, I seem to remember the taking advantage bit.'

'It's difficult to know who took advantage of who.' She reached across the table and caught my sleeve. 'God, Michael. I really missed you.'

The lights flashed on and off. Last orders. 'Oh shit,' I said. 'I've been out of Ireland for too long. I forgot about

37

these barbaric licensing laws. Do you want another one?'

She looked around. 'No. This place is way too noisy for a decent conversation. Come on back to my place. I have a bottle of plonk in the fridge.'

I smiled again. 'Sounds like a plan.'

Two hours and several drinks later we were sitting on a bench in her garden. I sipped my wine and watched the sky, feeling her eyes on the side of my face. She was quiet. A captive audience.

'I didn't make a conscious decision to become a pilgrim. It just happened. I used to detest the civil servants who milled around the top of O'Connell Street every Friday evening with bags full of dirty washing to take home to Mummy in Portumna. I never used to associate myself with the poor creature with the Kerry accent who had the misfortune to pass us in the pub.' I put the glass to my lips and took another sip, then looked at her sideways, a smile playing on my lips.

'What?' she said, laughing. She leaned against the arm of the bench, her legs drawn up beside her on the seat. She held her wineglass in both hands in front of her, like a chalice being offered. The arms of her sweater were pulled down around her hands, and her fingers, exposed, looked cold and pink against the glass.

'Do you know why they're called rednecks?' I asked. She shook her head. I slapped myself firmly on the back of the neck and roared, 'Get up to Dublin, get a job.'

She smiled and pushed my leg with her foot. 'That's awful. Jesus.'

We sat in silence for a moment, smiling, her foot resting against me.

'I mean, don't get me wrong,' I said. 'Germany isn't a bad place to live. It beats the hell out of here. But sometimes I just wake up in the morning and wonder if this is it. All the plans, the dreams. The things I'd do. The places I'd see. I've seen a lot of places, but scratch the surface and they're all the same really. It's people. People are different.' I was tired and emotional. I knew I was babbling, but I knew she didn't care. I had always babbled to her. 'I've missed you. All the long nights just sitting talking shite. It's good to see you.'

Her smile widened. 'It's good to see you too. Although, I'm still not sure why I'm bothering to talk to you.' She pushed against me again. 'You'll probably fly back tomorrow and I won't hear from you for another five years or so.'

I leaned against her, grinning. 'Probably. I won't make any promises . . . If memory serves me correctly, I seem to remember making a lot of promises before.'

'Yeah. You did.' For a moment her mood darkened. 'Anyway, forget it. I'm cold, let's go inside.' She started to stand up, but I put a hand on her arm and pulled her back down beside me.

'Hey, how many nights do you get to sit outside in Ireland? Let's stay a little longer.'

'Michael,' she said, exasperated. 'The feet are frozen off me.'

She wasn't wearing any shoes. She pulled her knees up to her chin and began to knead her feet. I touched her left foot. It was like ice. 'Here, let me.' I took her feet in my hands and started to rub them. 'Nice?'

'Mm.'

I slipped off my shoes and socks and pulled her towards me, facing away from her. I pulled a sock onto her left foot. She began to laugh. 'What are you doing?'

'Providing clothing for Madam's perished tootsies,' I said, in my best Jeeves accent.

She slipped her other leg around my waist. Her arms encircled me from behind. She stifled her laughter in my shoulder. I pulled the other sock on and put back on my own shoes. She was still holding me. 'I missed you too.'

I caught her hands and held them, rubbing warmth into them now. Her chin was on my shoulder. It was meant to be a brotherly kiss on the cheek. A simple gesture of affection. But her mouth was so warm and inviting. I could feel her breasts against my back. Our lips brushed. I twisted around and pushed her down on the bench. Hunger now. She responded, her tongue probing, darting, caressing. The signals had been there after all. Perhaps subconscious, but there. She was wrestling with my clothes now. Pulling frantically at my shirt. Pushing her hands inside, her fingers searching, scratching, skating across my chest. Her body arched towards me.

'Let's go inside.'

She led me across the garden and through the french doors to the kitchen. We stopped there, leaning against the worktop, discovering each other again. Touching, exploring. Then down the hall. She climbed four steps before I dragged her down, giggling, lay on top of her, and kissed her laughing mouth until she lay still. That is where I made love to her. Gentle, slow, unhurried.

I told her I loved her. I told her I had always loved her. We were in her bed. Four o'clock in the morning. She pushed herself up on her elbows and looked at me, tears in her eyes. She told me she was confused. She had been in love with me when I left. It had taken her so long to get over me. She didn't want to have to go through all that again.

'Don't,' I said. 'I love you. I've always loved you.'

It seemed like the right thing to say.

I went with them to Bride Street, morning Mass. I was, at best, a disinclined disciple, dragged from bed. Maria let me moan at first, then silenced me, a finger on my lips. 'Don't be selfish, Michael. This will be the first time she's seen anyone since the funeral. You should be there.' I ran my hand through my hair, snapped the elastic on my boxer shorts, sighed, and reluctantly agreed. I was needed. Immoral support.

My responses bore no resemblance to the right ones. I muttered them for Mother. I squirmed, fidgeted and yawned. Leaning against Maria, I whispered in her ear, 'I'd forgotten how boring this was.' She shushed me and pushed me away. The ceremony crept towards communion. My mother threw me a filthy look when it became obvious that I was not going to accompany her to the altar-rails. I already felt like a hypocrite. To waltz up the aisle would have been too much for me. I met her eye, belligerent, until she looked away, hoisted her handbag, and went without me. Maria followed her, sweeping from the seat, leaving me rubbing my hands together and staring at the floor.

Outside a plague of hands descended. Shaking. Holding. Touching. I stood, my mother's bodyguard, behind her, looking blank. I saw Claire climb into a car with her parents. She hesitated, looking at Maria deep in conversation with a nun, then blew a kiss across the car park. I smiled and turned away.

After lunch we packed and said goodbye. My mother held my hand and touched my face, her eyes shining, a film of tears. Her pain shocked me, the depth concealed until now. Being alone frightened her. I felt the burden of responsibility again.

'Come with us, Mother.' The words fell from me. I did not recognise the tenderness in my voice. Maria looked at me and nodded, smiling.

'No, Michael,' my mother said. 'But thanks for asking.'

We understood each other, finally. I would never stay and she could never go. We squeezed each other's hands. She seemed to straighten then, finding a reservoir of strength inside herself. New mood, she wiped a hand casually across her eyes, releasing me. 'Anyway, Germany is full of foreigners.' She stepped away. Alone. Alive.

In the car, I rolled down the window, looking at her standing stooped, hands clasped in front of her, as if in prayer. 'We'll be in touch, okay?'

'Yes.'

'I left a cheque beside the phone. In case you need it. Bills. You know.'

'That's kind. You shouldn't worry about these things.'

'It's okay. Honest. Listen. We'll see you soon.'

Frank started the engine. She put a hand on the door frame, leaning in. 'Goodbye, Maria. Thank you. Thanks for everything.'

Maria leaned over and kissed her. 'You take care.'

And then we left, like prisoners escaping, Frank stopping at Crosstown, the graveyard. It was Maria's idea.

– *You should say goodbye.*

– *He's dead, for Christ's sake.*

We stood beside the grave, still fresh, brown weal against green grass and gathered tombstones. Tuesday's flowers were withered in the sunlight. I stood beside Maria, her head bent in silent prayer, feeling numb. A little girl with pigtails put roses on a grave across the path, then skipped away, singing, followed by pensive parents.

'Come on. Let's go.' I walked away, sucking on my sunglasses. Maria followed me, reluctant. Then empty roads to Dublin were tunnels out of town. I began to breathe again.

When we got to the airport, Frank insisted on carrying Maria's bags to the check-in desk. He stood awkwardly beside us in the queue, shuffling forward at every opportunity, like a child excited to be travelling.

'How many travelling?' the ground stewardess asked.

'Just two.'

Frank shifted his feet and looked at the floor. 'I'll go wait over there then.'

Maria kissed him on the cheek before we headed for the boarding gate. I watched him turn bright red, a smile playing on my lips. 'Goodbye, Frank. And thanks again.' I took his hand in mine. His handshake was not as firm as I remembered. I thought of times when, as a child, his grip was like a vice that crushed my fingers. He came to help my father once. They built a garden shed. I marvelled at this giant of a man. His strength. He could throw bricks around as if they only weighed the same as lego. He was the biggest, strongest man on earth. I noticed, for the first time, that I was two or three inches taller than him.

He threw an arm around my neck and hugged me, embarrassed. 'God bless you, Michael.' His eyes were full of tears.

'We'll see you, Frank.'

'Please God. Please God.'

He stood, car keys in hand, watching us as we made our way through security. I looked back before we turned the corner. There he was, framed by the metal detector, his once powerful hand, now crippled with arthritis, waving solemnly. I thought to myself how transient we are.

# Amongst Women

I was a serious child. Bowed beneath the worries of the world. Teachers gave us green dog-tags, scapulars. *If you aren't wearing this when you die, you'll go straight to Hell.* I need to know more. Do I go to Heaven if I am? *Of course.* Michael breaks his scapular trying to hang himself. Explain that . . . Imagine that . . . Girls are taught by celibate nuns. *Sit on his knee and you'll get pregnant.* Insult a child's intelligence, why don't you? *At least put a telephone directory between you.* Irish contraception? Land of my youth. *Sex is dirty.* Learn about it in the school yard. Brother or son? Mother and child. Why did you not know better? *Don't talk about it, it will never happen. Don't look at it, it will go away.*

'I'm late.'

'Not to worry. What are you having?' Maria has just walked into the pub.

'Worry. And it's a little too early to say.'

'What?' I am confused at first, then it dawns on me. My face drops.

'Give the man a Pfennig.'

'How late?'

'Late enough. A bastard. Like father like son.'

Christ, Maria, talk to me. Drop the anger, just for a minute. I want to shake her. What are you saying? What's happening? How? 'Are you sure?'

'Of course I'm sure. I wouldn't have said anything if I wasn't sure.' She stands in front of me, arms folded. 'I saw the doctor today. Seven weeks, he reckons. I wanted to know for certain before I told you.'

'Jesus, how long . . . ?'

'Yes, I knew before.'

'Why didn't you . . . ?'

'Tell you? Would it have changed anything? Not really. You might have tried, Michael, but a leopard can't change his spots. You might even have thought I was just trying to trap you.'

I sit in silence, fingering my pint glass. She's right of course. She had called that morning, before I left for work. *The Shamrock, six o'clock.* A lifeline? Both ends, it turns out. News which would have made me ecstatic two months ago now threatens to devour me. It sinks in. Slowly at first, then with a suddenness that terrifies me. The child I always wanted, but by a women that I have taught to hate me. This child will surely hate me too. Oh sweet Jesus. Is nothing ever simple in this world?

'Sit down, Maria. Please.' She sits, stiff, the table between us, the strap of her handbag wound around her arm. 'What are we going to do?'

'We?' She glares at me. 'It's me who's having the baby, Michael.'

*I might have had something to do with it too.* Temper, Michael, temper. 'I just mean, have you thought about what to tell people? What about us? Shouldn't we talk about our future?'

She snorts, as if this is a joke. 'We haven't got a future, Michael. You made sure of that. This doesn't change anything between you and me.'

'Okay then.' I hold my hands out to her, palms extended. 'What are *you* going to do?'

'I'm going back to Ireland at the end of the month. I've already resigned. Today. I told my mother. She says I'm welcome to come home for as long as I want.'

'You could come back to me.'

'Cop yourself on, Michael.'

'Sorry. I just . . . Sorry.' I know that I deserve this. For what I've done. I chew at a hangnail for a moment, wondering where to go from here. I reach across the table for her, but she pulls her hand away. 'You never did want to raise a German, did you?' I smile at her. 'Going back to Ireland is probably for the best. Is there anything I can do to help?'

'No.'

'Come on, have a drink. Let's talk about it.'

'You're the last person in the world I want to talk to right now, Michael.' She's gathering her things.

'I love you.'

She looks at me. Incredulous. I don't know if she will laugh, cry, or spit in my face. 'Fuck off, Michael.' And then she is gone, banging the door behind her.

I could follow her, force her to see reason. But whose reason? Mine? Besides, I can't move. A giant hand is holding me in place, crushing the air from my lungs. A child? My child? Yes and no. My flesh and blood. But I will not see the first step, hear the first word. This child will never call me Daddy, will wonder who it is that sends the presents. This child will not carry my name, but I will carry its existence for the rest of my life. Maria, how can you tell me this changes nothing? It doesn't feel as though nothing has changed.

Remember us? Afraid to make a sound. German rules. No noise after ten. Irish again. Tinkers. *I couldn't give a shite.* Large lungs, larynx loud. There'll be hell to pay tomorrow. Or today. I am a madman after midnight. Cold beneath this argument, you huddle in a chair. All misty-eyed and mystified. *I'm losing you, amn't I?* A trembling lip can give away a thought.

'Michael. Stop. Please.'

But your words will just incense me, like worms, winding through my flesh, feeding. Haven't you seen this impatience grow in me? Can't you tell that I want out?

'Michael.' A hoarse whisper, shaking, your face boiled red and wrinkled with emotion. 'The neighbours.'

Trust you to think of that. Of them. I'm drowning here. *Drowning, for fuck's sake.*

'Michael.' Shriek. Hands fly to cover ears, protect them from my ranting. Knees pulled tight against your chest. Head. Bent. Low. In supplication. Face hidden behind golden hair, your tears drop, drenching bare feet. Something stalls me, halting, hanging mouth. Your toes. Curled. Tense against the fabric of the chair. So small. Like a child's. *Thoughts of them, meeting you on the stairs tomorrow, laden, maybe, with washing for the cellar. Stares. And they will smile. All false, looking for bruises. Guten Morgen. None. How disappointing. But tongues will wag, regardless. I am suddenly ashamed. Something to do with your toes. Does that make sense?* Enough. I sink against the wall, shoulders rocking, burying my own face. My hands are clenched claws, my fingertips, solid on my skin, bury themselves like needles in my scalp. Christ. This can't go on.

You find me there and pull me to the surface, kneeling, gentle hands. Butterfly kisses on wet cheeks. 'Michael. Come on. It's okay.' Is it?

'I'm sorry, Maria.' Mouth wide, saliva-stained, I let you hold my head against your breast. You are mother now. Minding.

'Shh. Everything is going to be all right.'

But I know things you don't, Maria. I know who I am. And I know what I've done.

'So sorry.' Child. Whimpering.

Claire today. On the telephone.

*– So if you're so unhappy, why don't you leave her?*

Simple? Maybe. But after all this time . . .

'It's okay. It's okay. I understand.' You pat my back, arms wrapped tight around me, holding me, keeping me from harm. But you will never understand.

*– I mean, honestly, Michael, if it's not right it's not right. You'd be better to end it now . . .*

You place a hand on each of my flushed cheeks, pulling my head around and looking into my eyes. 'Michael, I know how upset you are. I know what it's like to lose your father. Mine died when I was young. It's okay. You can talk to me. Trust me, for God's sake. Talk to me.'

*– You just have to tell her, Michael.*

'I can't.'

'Why not, Michael? Just when I think things are finally going right, you retreat again. Back into that shell of yours. And I find myself living with a stranger. It's not good enough. We're supposed to be a team, you know. Helping each other through the rough times. You know?'

'Yeah, I know.' Your hands are cold against me. *Warm heart.* Soothing. 'It's just hard. I do trust you.' *Don't trust me.* 'I'm just not sure what I want to say. I don't even know what I think at the moment.'

*– Just tell her.*

You smile. Painful for you. 'I have to say, Michael, when things are good between us they're pretty good. But when they're bad I could kill you. Things have been pretty bad for the past few weeks.'

*– Nobody said it was going to be easy.*

'I know how selfish I've been. Don't think I don't. This isn't easy. I'm a private person. You know that. Sometimes I find it hard having somebody around all the time. Like now. I need time. To sort some things out. You know? Then maybe I can explain. Do you know what I mean?'

'Oh, Michael.' You sigh and slump against the wall beside me, sitting on your heels. 'I understand. Of course I do. But how long is it going to take before you let me in? I don't know how much more of this I can take.' You lean your forehead against a tiny fist. 'Your father is dead, Michael. I can't change that. You can't change it. You have to get on with your life. Whatever this guilt trip you're on is, it's time to let it go.'

*— It's time to let her go.*

'That's about it all right. Guilt trip.' My head is pounding, temples throbbing, pressure. 'I'm guilty, Maria. How could I be any other way?' You look at me and touch my arm. 'My father is dead, Maria. I think the last time we spoke we argued. Shit, I can't even remember the last time we spoke. How do you think that makes me feel?'

'I don't know what to tell you.'

I bite a knuckle, hot pain holding back the tears. 'I thought . . . I suppose I thought that sooner or later we'd resolve things. You know? Sort it all out? But I kept putting it on the long finger. Kept waiting. Putting it off. Only now it's too late. How the fuck do you think that makes me feel?'

'Oh, Michael.'

I can feel hot tears stinging my eyes again. 'I didn't cry at the funeral. I can imagine them all, what they thought. *Hard bastard. He doesn't give a shit.* And do you know what the worst thing is?'

You look at me, eyes soft with tears, and shake your head.

'I haven't learned a fucking thing. Not a thing. He's dead. And I'm here, sitting in Germany, crying, for fuck's sake, and I'm still barely on speaking terms with my mother. Oh Christ. It's fucking hopeless.'

You squeeze my arm, compassionate. If only you knew

what else was on my mind. But I avoid that.

'Michael. Come here. Come on.' You hold me close again. I can hear your heart beating next to my ear, feel a tear trickling down my cheek and dripping onto my forearm. 'Go a bit easy on yourself,' you say. 'You're not the hard bastard you think you are.' I pull away from you, sniffing and rubbing at my eyes, fighting back the tears. 'Oh, Michael,' your hands are on my shoulders now, 'why don't you just let it all out.'

You kneel in front of me and pull me towards you. Suddenly I am sobbing uncontrollably, face buried in your shoulder. You hold me tight and tell me everything is going to be all right. I want to believe you. Need to believe you. Your tee-shirt smells fresh and clean, your breasts nuzzle my chest. I cling to you like a baby, suckling. I am aware of your tiny waist and I feel a familiar tenderness, afraid to squeeze too hard in case I break the fragile flower in my arms. Soft kisses on my neck, I look for you. Your lips touch mine and I am intoxicated by you. I slip a hand inside your tee-shirt, feel your back, spine sprinkled like the Pyrenees, bisecting soft, cool skin. A whiteness I cannot resist. I move my hand under your skirt and along the inside of your sylph-like leg. You catch it, stopping me, and look into my eyes. 'No.' A whisper. Gentle. 'Just hold me.'

And I hold you, pressing myself to you, kissing your hair. 'I love you.'

*– Just tell her . . .*

A light turns red. All stop.

Paused. Suspended. Waiting. Engines gunned around us. We are part of something. Animal. Straining at a leash.

I look at you, perspiration playing on your face, your skirt pulled up around your thighs, exhausted from the heat. You turn to me and smile, blowing a drop of sweat from the end of your nose.

What would happen if I left you now? Just walked away,

engine idling, leaving you gasping like a goldfish. Pedestrians would peer through open windows. Angry motorists would lean on horns, cursing in frustration. And you, shocked, would watch me shrinking in the crowd.

I could do it. Drop out of gear and step from the car. I can see it. *Michael, where are you going?* You would lean across the handbrake, asking through the open door. Confused. And I would not look back. So easy. I *could* do it.

This is a strange city. I would vanish here. Like Amelia. Gone. A ghost.

You are talking. I can see your lips move. Asking, perhaps, why I look so strange. No sound comes. I am miles away. Walking. Things will never be the same. I have already done it. Liberated. I am gone.

My hand inches towards the gear-stick. I can feel the excitement build in me. So many things undiscovered. Unburdened, I will start again. Anonymous.

'Michael. The light is green.'

A light is green. Go. Move on. A chance gone begging. Move.

In days to come, I will drive past this street corner. I will gaze along that road, past green trees and parked cars. Wondering.

*Some wounds we inflict are unintentional. Callous words, thrown incautiously. A minor indiscretion. Or two. Some hurt will heal. Forgiven, we breathe again. Proceed. And, after faltering steps, we learn to walk again. But some scars ache eternally. I cannot pretend that I was unaware of this. Cannot claim ignorance. Her face, twisted, haunts me now. The pain cannot be hidden. Some cuts run too deep. Poor child.*

I sat on the edge of the bed, contemplating my running shoes. Maria was in the kitchen, always an early riser. I plucked a magazine from the bedside table and leafed through it, reading the first two or three lines of an article, then flicking to another page. Eventually I sighed, threw the magazine on the bed, and pulled on my shoes, not bothering to lace them up. I shuffled into the kitchen. She looked up from a cookery book, steaming coffee cup beside her, seated, elbow resting on the worktop, buttered toast in her hand. She swallowed, smiled, bid me good morning.

'Any preferences for dinner?' Chirpy.

'Christ, I haven't even had breakfast.' I poured myself some coffee, sniffing at it. Strong. 'Fuck me, I'm bolloxed.'

'Good morning to you too.' A smile in her voice.

'Sorry, hangover.' A good excuse not to talk.

'I thought maybe veal.' She was trying, always trying.

'Whatever.'

Silence. My point.

I stood with my back to her, looking out the window. The sun was shining. Bright. Light bouncing from the street below us, showering white splinters into my tired eyeballs. We had been back a month. July now. It had not been the easiest of months. I came back to Germany determined, if that's not too strong a word, to start afresh. *Okay, so you got sucked back in briefly. Forget it.* Ireland was a bad smell. It followed you around for a while, but if you left it alone for long enough it would go away, dissipate. *If she needs me she'll call.* Kathleen Dwyer wasn't like that though. She would let me stew in my own juice. Physically I could walk away, but she knew that she would haunt my dreams.

Years had knocked the corners off my relationship with Maria. Delicate sculpture. Chip away, one piece at a time, reveal the beauty in the stone. One mistake. *Can't have a face without a nose, boy.* One heavy-handed hammer blow, one slip, one moment of weakness. Claire. Nothing for it but to start again. But I didn't know if that was what I wanted. A month now of constant bickering and fighting. Maria was confused at first. She put it down to my being upset about my father's death. She did everything she could to help me. To make things easy for me. The more she tried the more difficult I became. We sank into an uneasy silence. Truce? No. Not really. The war raged silently.

Dark spaces appeared in our relationship. Empty silences. Vacuum. I withdrew. Slowly. Painfully. Lazy Sunday afternoons grew cold and distant. She watched and waited, making no demands. She sensed the precipice as I tottered on the brink, afraid to snatch me back in case she inadvertently pushed me over the edge. We grew apart with far greater speed than we had grown together. Perhaps it only took an instant. A nanosecond to define a lifetime. Two lifetimes. Michael makes a choice. Drops the stone that starts the ripples. *Do the waves make you tired, Maria? Shame on me. You should do something about it.* But she stayed. She clutched at straws. She didn't stop loving me.

I sipped my coffee, she read her cookery book. A meal for me. Another olive branch. I would not like it. I had become predictable. Despicable. Like a tide, she would come towards me. Unyielding, rock, I stood my ground until, energy spent, she would retreat.

'Do you want to come shopping?' she tried again.

'No. I'm going for a run.'

'Why don't you come to town? We could go for a swim later.'

'No. I want to run.'

I turned around, catching a glimpse of frustration before she managed to control her face.

'Okay.' A weak smile. Eyes sorrowful, hurt.

I poured the last of my coffee into the sink and showed the cup to running cold water. She would wash it with her breakfast things when I was gone. I took an apple from the fruit bowl, rinsed it, and headed for the door. 'See you later.'

'Bye.' She sounded sad, her composure crumbling. She started every day as if this would be the one. The day when we would pick up where we left off, falling asleep in each other's arms having made love, before a phone call shattered our happiness. I didn't turn around. I didn't tell her what I knew. I didn't tell her not to keep on waiting for a day that wouldn't come. I didn't tell her that I had not been happy. Not even then.

She must have watched me leave. Broad back. Shoulders stooped. Brooding presence. Moving away. Through the open doorway. Into the hall. Kneeling. Shoelaces. Standing. Stretching. Vanishing. Door. Closing. Gone.

When my father died nothing changed. I expected something dramatic, some enlightenment. Some bolt of lightning. He left nothing. An emptiness that disappeared along with the image of my mother, standing in her doorway, waving goodbye. When I try now, perhaps I can recall an instant when I caught a glimpse of my own soul. Perhaps he did try to show me the mistakes that I would make. Perhaps he did try to pass his life-force to me, to make me into the man he was . . . But no. I don't believe in ghosts.

He died so many times for me. A child winning a race and knowing that it is because he can. A cruel youth using the education paid for by another's sweat to expose an ignorance. Embarrassment. Inconvenience. How could this man's death change me? I had erased him so completely from my life that I could not accurately recall the details of his face, the tone of his voice. I knew that I should feel pain, so I felt pain. But when it was no longer required I switched it off. I denied it. I made it go away. I had told my mother that I could not just leave it all behind. I believed it when I said it, but that is exactly what I did. I went back to Germany and left it all behind. I chastised myself for my moments of weakness and sent the odd cheque to ease my troubled conscience.

I ran, sweat streaking my face. *Thump, thump.* Methodical footfalls. The sun beat down on my back. Unbearable. I entered the coolness of the forest. Shade, hills, roots to trip you, leaves to slip on. Other runners passed me by. *Morgen.* Stranger's smile. *Thump, thump.* Heartbeat. My breathing grew shallow. Routine. This used to bring me peace. Not now. Faces swam before my eyes. My mother, Maria, Claire. *Thump, thump.* Measured pace. Keep going.

She answered on the sixth ring. Breathless, as if she had been running too. I let her say hello three times before I spoke. I pictured her, dark hair falling over the phone, panting, chest rising, falling. Expression clouding. *Who's this heavy breather on the line?*

'Claire?'

'Michael? Hi.' Relief. Happy that it's me, and not just any pervert.

'I want to see you.'

'What? Where are you?'

'Germany. Come over.'

She paused. 'What about what's her name?'

'Maria? It's like I said in the letter. It's all over bar the shouting. Granted, there's been a lot of shouting. I need to see you. Come on. I'll take you away for a dirty weekend. What do you say?'

'I don't know, Michael. I'm not sure how I feel about all this.' Reluctance in her voice.

'Just do it, okay? I'll book the ticket. Just name the day.'

'Oh, Michael.' Pleading. 'Let me think about it.'

'Say yes.'

'No.' Laughing.

'Say yes, Claire.'

'Okay. Yes, Claire.'

'Does that mean you'll come?'

'Well if I go all the way to Germany for a dirty weekend and I don't come, you're in big trouble, buster.'

'Tell you what. Get over here next weekend and I'll see what I can do.'

'I'll bet you will. It's a date.'

Later, I stayed in the shower for a long time. I stood, legs apart, arms braced against the sides of the cubicle, and lifted my face to the water. *You're a shithead, Dwyer. What the fuck do you think you're at?* Too late for qualms of conscience. Claire was ripe with possibilities and I wanted her. I needed something to pull me out of this hole that I had been digging for myself. Somebody, please, upset the applecart.

She looked good. Tanned face, white teeth, brown hair, blue jeans. We didn't say hello, I just took her in my arms and kissed her. Intense, deep, passionate kisses, we were locked together in the middle of a jostling, bustling crowd of holidaymakers in the arrivals hall. She laughed when I finally let her surface.

'I guess you're pleased to see me then. Or is that a gun in your pocket?' I just grinned at her, the cat that got the cream. 'Aren't you afraid someone will see you?'

'Fuck 'em.' I took her bag and hoisted it over my shoulder. 'Your chariot awaits, Madame.'

We walked together, arms wrapped around each other, like Siamese twins. I didn't even try to conceal anything. I suppose I wanted to be found out. Some stupid excuse about wanting to get away on my own for a couple of days. *I'm just going to drive and see where I end up.* She must have known. She has to have known. She said nothing. Hurt hidden, sealed lips, veiled eyes. She let me go. As I recall, she even packed a bag for me.

Dearest Maria. You didn't deserve an asshole like me. You really should have had better.

'For Christ's sake, Maria.' Bellow. A voice from the past.

*For Christ's sake, Kate.* Warm edges of sleep. A child in the dark. Fuzzy, dreamy, bedroom. The fresh smell of childhood sheets. Rain tap-tapping on the window. Jack Frost come to bite my nose? Door ajar, soft light creeps across the floor and climbs into bed with me. The pillow tastes marshmallow warm. Muffled voices. Familiar first. Comfortable, cosy. Wait. Tiny brow wrinkles. Something here that frightens. Sinister. Breath catches. Wrenched from deepest sleep. Simple dreams banished. Shadows threaten. Troubled child. *Daddy? DADDY!* Angry voices hang in midair, silenced by a frightened child. I can hear his footsteps growing louder. She is sobbing quietly. *Go to sleep. What's happening? Everything's all right. Go to sleep.* And, being a child, I slept. Trusting. Blind faith. Everything is all right. Best forgotten. All forgotten. Until now.

*For Christ's sake, Maria.* A hand hangs above me. Mine? I don't remember raising it. I stare at it for a moment, incredulous. She has stepped back, shrunken into herself, eyes closed, face screwed up, waiting for me to rain down blows. Believing I am capable of that. *Michael?* It's me asking. *Are you capable of that?* Time freezes, like a rabbit caught in a car's headlights. I feel like I am underwater. Everything has a strange, otherworldly feel. And then it is as if I have broken through a barrier. Time rights itself. Suddenly my hand is propelled forward as if by some unseen force. The impact jars me, pain's fiery fingers caress my knuckles and engulf my arm to the elbow. The trance ends. I turn on my heel, pick my coat off the floor where I have thrown it and go out into the rain, leaving her staring at the spot on the wall where I have spent my anger.

The car slips through empty streets like a thief in the night. Knife. Sliding straight and smooth through murky water. The big engine seems silent, rubber tyres velvet against rain-soaked roads. I am calm now. Shifting gears seamlessly, I glide away from traffic lights. Frankfurt's streets glisten, neon light reflecting, ruptured by soft summer rain. Shop fronts flash by. A prostitute at a bus shelter near Kaiser Straße blows a kiss through my window as I turn a corner. The windscreen wipers swat away beads of rain. Cow tails whipping at flies.

I park in a cul-de-sac near Sachsenhausen. The stereo is

still playing. Loud music washing over me. I sit for a while. Silence. Breathing. Nostrils flared. Get control of yourself, man. My left hand rests on the steering wheel. I look at it. Detached. Swollen knuckles skinned and bloody. I lift it, turn it, examine it, flex it. Nothing broken. Bruising nicely though.

I don't feel like drinking any more. I don't feel like anything. I sigh and turn the key in the ignition. *Time to go home, Michael.*

She is still sitting in the hallway when I return. Slumped against the wall, legs crossed, hair across her dirty, tear-stained face. Urchin. *Penny for the baby.* Suddenly I am filled with love, loss, guilt, repentance. Anything. I want to stop this. Tell her that I love her. Take her in my arms. *I am so sorry, Maria.*

Instead, I say, 'Go to bed, for fuck's sake.'

She looks at me from under her tangled fringe. Is that what hate looks like? Smothering a sob, she stands up, slowly. She says nothing, but her eyes never leave mine. Defiant. I look away first. Then she turns and walks slowly into the bedroom, closing the door behind her. I hear the key turn in the lock. Barrier.

*'Jaysus, would you ever hurry up with me Access?'*

*I wonder what it is that precipitates this tendency to inject the word 'Jaysus' into even the most mundane sentence. I never used to swear. But now it seems I can't resist the temptation to utilise every opportunity to insult both saints and scholars. She looks at me, coldly, as she swipes the card. A pen is proffered, and I sign. Practised flourish. Michael Dwyer. Collecting my credit card and twelve-year-old Jameson, I saunter towards the boarding gate with the arrogance of the seasoned traveller. I have become a pilgrim.*

*'Last call for flight EI 653 to Dublin.'*

*Last call me arse. Once they have your bag there's no way they'll leave without you.*

*'Mr Dwyer, travelling to Dublin, please go to gate E7 immediately . . .'*

*. . . I go.*

*On the bus everything is noise, sweat and baggage. I hold my bags, afraid they will be trampled. Knotted muscles complain bitterly. The trip across the tarmacadam seems to last forever. Red-faced people wrapped in woollen clothes are trapped, like cattle, breathing biohazard close. We stand together, glazed, we are a herd. Sunlight streaming through the window, weak, begins a deluge underneath my arm that trickles slowly down my back. Tickling sweat, armpit aware, I hold my arms pressed tight against my sides.*

*At last we board, luggage laden, shuffling along the aisle, like prisoners on a chain gang. I find my place and sit with English papers. Ignored, an air hostess stands close to me. Safety semaphore makes travellers uneasy. But then again, we've heard it all before.*

*After take-off, the hum of the engines becomes hypnotic. I am not able to concentrate on my newspaper. If I hold it, though, my neighbour can finish off the article he's reading. To hell with that. I fold it, sitting on the sports page, expecting him to ask me if I am reading it.*

*My eyelids are heavy. I watch wisps of cloud flit past the window. The 'no smoking' light winks off and the air hostesses spring to life. They will soon be here with my gin-and-tonic. I rub at my eyes, stretch, yawn and succumb to the inevitable. To sleep, perchance to dream . . .*

Claire shakes me. 'Coffee?'

'Wha . . . ? Oh. Yeah.' I sit up in her bed, eyes sandy, tongue glued to the roof of my mouth. 'What time is it?'

'Time you got up if you want to get to Dublin in time to catch your plane.' She is wearing my shirt, long legs descending. She sits on the edge of the bed, curling one leg under her. I catch a glimpse of pubic hair. She leans forward, one too many buttons open. Cleavage. 'Good afternoon.' She kisses me. Fresh, clean breath. I am conscious of my own stale, beer and garlic stink. I keep my mouth closed, unresponsive. She stays bent forward, one breast falling loose, china white, ruby nipple. She cups it in her hand, pouting, little girl face. Moistening her forefinger in her mouth, she traces rings around her nipple. I watch it swell and harden. 'Don't you want to play today?' I can feel myself stiffen.

'I have a plane to catch.' She kneels on the bed, dark hair tumbling across her face, playful, gathering the quilt in her hands, exposing my lower belly. I clutch at the sheet, covering myself. She begins to lick my stomach, tongue making long languorous loops around my naval. I put my hands on the sides of her head and lift her face up where I can see it. 'Plane?'

She looks at me salaciously, under drooping eyelids. 'Relax, lover boy. I said it was time to get up, not to get out of bed.' I let her go. She has worked her hands under the covers. She begins to kiss my stomach again. I put my hands behind my head, holding on to the headboard, and give in to her.

'Like I said,' I say as she takes me in her mouth, 'I had a plane to catch.'

A weekend by water. Last chance? I sit, solitary, listening to waves. She has deafened me with silence. She is here now. Eyes. Danger. Guard them, they give away too much. Struggles to the surface, swims in blue pools. Go back, drown there. Too strong. Or I'm too weak. Too late. There. Now you know. Don't you?

She is staring at me. 'Well?'

'Huh? Did you say something? Sorry, I was a million miles away.'

'I noticed.'

Someone in the next room coughs. There is a tension between us that has grown and festered for some time now. She stands, staring. I sit. Neither speaks. Eyes locked. I am convinced she knows what I've been thinking. I shift slightly, look away, out to sea.

'Michael.' Softly. 'We can't go on like this. If you want me to go, I will.'

I don't answer at first. Tears are stinging my eyes. They are not for her. They are for me. She walks around me, sees that I am crying.

'What's wrong? God, why won't you talk to me?'

'I'm sorry.'

'For what?'

And then she knows. All of a sudden. She has peeled back my scalp, cracked my skull and looked into my mind. She does not like what she sees there, what I have hidden from her. My guilty secret.

'You want me to go. Don't you?'

'Yes.'

There it is. Out now. Ejaculated. I couldn't hold it any longer.

She blinks. The person in the next room coughs again. She can't believe what she has heard. Or rather, she can, but does not want to. A single tear slips quietly from the corner of her right eye and moves down her cheek in slow motion. I cannot take my eyes off it. It passes her mouth, slowly, slowly. I watch the tiny drop cling to her chin, struggling against gravity, fighting to stay with her. If I'm fast enough I can catch it. I don't move. It can't hold on any longer. I watch it turn, topple, fall, open-mouthed, silent scream. It shatters on my shoe. I watch its dark blood blossom on the brown leather. She has not moved. I see myself through her eyes, vision fly-like, fragmented by unshed tears. Hundreds of me, all staring at our shoes. Is this what all these tears are for, Maria? How many will you cry for me?

I drag my eyes upward, defiant, meet her gaze. She is looking through me, her mind elsewhere. She opens her mouth, about to speak, but cannot make a sound. Her mouth closes again. Snap. *Michael, you're a fucking bastard.* Go on. Say it. Please. For me. She turns, slowly, makes her way across the room. Like a sleepwalker. She opens the wardrobe and takes out her suitcase.

'What are you doing?'

'Packing.'

'You don't have to go tonight.'

'Yes, I do.' She is carefully folding her clothes now.

'Don't be silly. Where will you stay? How will you get back to Frankfurt?'

'I'll get a train. Or something.'

'For God's sake, Maria.' I get out of my chair and come in from the balcony.

'Please don't come near me, Michael.' She has stopped moving now. She is very calm. For a moment I think she has even stopped breathing. 'Do you really think I could stay with you now? For even one night?'

'I'll go then. It's my fault.'

'No. I couldn't stay here. Not now.'

'We have to talk about this.'

'What is there to say? When you get back to Frankfurt I'll give you a call and arrange to pick up my things. Could you go out for a few minutes, please? I need to finish packing.'

This is not what I expected. Curse me. Throw a fit. Hit me. Scream. Kick. Damn my soul to Hell. She is standing perfectly still. Her right hand rests on her suitcase on the bed, her pale blue sweater is dangling from her left. I want to say something but I cannot think of what to say. Instead, I do as she asks. I take the room-key off the dressing table and go out, making my way to the hotel bar. When I come back she is gone. There is no note. Her clothes have all been removed from the wardrobe. I go to the bathroom. Nothing. No evidence of her. Calmly, coolly, with a strength I did not expect from her, she has removed herself from this place.

At first I want to go after her. What will she do? Where will she go? But no. She speaks the language. There's a late train. She'll call someone. She'll be okay. If I go after her it will only make things worse. This is what I wanted. Isn't it? Why didn't she rant and rave and scream at me?

I close the curtains to the balcony and take off my clothes. I drop them on the floor. She wouldn't have let me do that. I climb into bed. We made love here this afternoon. I put my face against her pillow. I can smell her perfume. The tears come again. I try to hold them back. They squeeze through, just a few at first, then more and more as my resolve dissolves. Deluge. My chest heaves. Can't stop. Great racking sobs. What have I done? What have I done? Maria. Oh Jesus, what will poor Michael do now?

'I'm late,' she says, standing in the Shamrock. And then she leaves me, mouth open, staring at the floor. It doesn't feel as though nothing has changed. Everything has changed.

*Dear Maria,*

*I tried to call this evening. Got as far as picking up the
phone. It's not the first time, it probably won't be the last.
What would I say if you answered? Poised, like a boxer, I
caught myself in time. Ready for an argument, steeled, I
stopped. We've had too much of that already.*

*There is so much that I need to say to you, so much left
unsaid. I'm becoming an expert at this, leaving everything
until it is too late. When I run through conversations in my
head, I hear my voice come calm and cool. Careful measured
stanzas. My dignity astounds me. Maturity in me. And clarity
of thought. Amazing in the face of such emotion . . . But in
reality you don't play by the rules, Maria. At least not my
rules.*

*That's why I write these letters. Even when you were here
I wrote, sat up late at night. You snored in the next room,
oblivious, while I poured my heart out on the page. At first I
meant to show you. 'Look. At last. A train of thought. For
you. Look.' But dawn dispelled my midnight madness, causing
me to think again. And thinking I would pause. And pausing
I would lose the chance. And lost, it's gone forever. A new day
renders obsolete obsessions of the former. Suffice it to say, my
dear Maria, I speak to you more often than you know.*

*I didn't know about the child. If I had it would be different.
When I think about it, though, it must be said, it could be for
the best. This is honest. This is true. You are not left
wondering. 'Duty, Michael? Duty's child? Do you really love
me?' Unencumbered, I was free. Free to make a choice, and I
have chosen.*

*There are days, Maria, or bits of days, when you crawl
beneath my skin. Inconsolable, I long for you, like a dog,
pining. The truth. You'd laugh at that. But don't. Believe. I
would not lie to you, not here in black and white. Another of
my rules.*

*So where to now, this love of ours? I am desolate without you. Steeped in saccharated self-absorption, I know the fool I am, or must appear. Perhaps you're just a phantom pain, like a limb, lopped off but not forgotten. But how can I forget? Insidious, you live inside of me. Parasite, unwanted, you have burrowed deep and I have grown accustomed to your presence. Does it feel the same to you? Or are you sitting somewhere now, washing your hands, saying, 'Good riddance, him I can live without!'?*

*A million thoughts teem inside my head, Maria. Careering off each other like wildly excited molecules. A thousand questions, jostling for pole position. What if? What if? What if? And do you know something, Maria? I have just recently realised that I don't have a single answer. We are soon to be parents. Separated. That bothers me more than you can know. Our father, who art in Germany? Not the most satisfactory of situations. Not much for a child to have faith in. But there is no simple solution, is there? What you want from me I cannot give. It seems that if you could you would swallow me, bones and all. There would be nothing left of me, no scrap, no morsel. Oh, Maria, you should know. You of all people. I need all of me for me. And there's the crux of it. I think of you, Maria. I think of our unborn child. But I can't stop thinking of myself. Swallow me bones and all? I think not. There are only crumbs for you.*

*I tried to call tonight, Maria. I tried. Instead I wrote a letter. A letter I will not send. More thoughts left unspoken. But what do you expect from me? I am, after all, a selfish bastard. But I do love you. Really.*

*Michael*

# VISITATIONS

*In my dream we are old. Our breath hangs against winter landscapes. We are black shadows on white snow. Negative. Picture postcard. Icicles cling to tree branches. The cold is punctuated by grandchildren's laughter. Through mittens your hand is warm in mine. I can feel your smile. We slip and slide together towards snowball fights. Small hands, turned snowman red, reach for elderly embraces. We are happy to oblige. We are happy. Happy. Far from now.*

*What should I tell you? How I wake mornings, afraid to open my eyes? Safe in the warm womb of the covers, pillow at my cheek, I keep my eyes tight shut, knowing that to open them is to lose you all over again.*

I took the plunge. Unannounced. Homecoming. I balanced my bag on a hip and reached up to the knocker. It wouldn't do to just walk in on her. Apart from anything else, she didn't know I had a key. There had been so much ado about giving me one for my twenty-first birthday. Years ago. A memory. Big fuss in front of friends. Major presentation. My father, shaking hands with me, showed the key with its red ribbon to the gathered masses. He leaned towards me, kissed my cheek, and whispered in my ear, 'I want that back.' But I made a copy before returning it and never told them. I never used it. Having it seemed to be enough. A gesture. Miniature rebellion.

She appeared in the doorway, wiping her hands in a dishcloth, a puzzled expression on her face as she let the door swing open. For an instant I caught her unguarded, older than her years. Grey face to match grey hair. Her mouth was a black line. A straight slit, like a posthumous wound, scalpel thin. Watery blue eyes were sunken lakes against a wrinkled vista. She jumped when she saw me. Startled. Then her face lit up, her eyes and mouth smiling a welcome.

'Michael. I don't believe it.' As if I was a ghost.

'How are you, Mother?'

'Come in, come in. Lord almighty. Where did you come from?' She reached for my face, her hands still damp from washing up, standing on tiptoes to kiss me. She was trembling. There were tears in her eyes. 'When did you get home?'

'This morning.'

A cloud crossed her face. 'Why didn't you call me? I would have gone up to Dublin to meet you.'

I smiled at her. 'Sure, what's the point in dragging you all the way up there. I caught the train.'

'It wouldn't have been any trouble. You should have called.'

'Then it wouldn't have been a surprise, Mother.'

'Well, I'm surprised.' She was beaming, clammy hands still on my cheeks. 'Oh, Michael. It's so good to see you.'

She led me into the kitchen, telling me there was a fresh pot of tea. I sat at a pine table I hadn't seen before and watched her cut slices of cheese for me.

'The table is new.'

She looked up. 'Yes. We needed one for ages, but you know how your father was. He insisted the old one was fine.' She smiled, her eyes far away. 'Didn't want to change.'

He had been like that towards the end. Carefully meticulous. Everything had its place. He would become flustered at the slightest variation to his routine. He clung to the familiar, like a drowning man.

Her lunch things rested on the draining board, a reminder of her interrupted chore. One cup, one plate, one knife, one teaspoon. Otherwise, the kitchen was ominously tidy. Sterile.

It took a while to work out what was missing. There had always been a bunch of flowers on the windowsill. The space looked strangely bare now, like a fresh haircut glimpsed in a bathroom mirror. Perhaps it had been him who brought them from the garden each day. Unsuspected romance, spanning years. Covert. Never mentioned. A secret shared between them. *He loved you, Mother. Didn't he?* She followed my gaze, her eyes resting on the empty windowsill for a moment. A faint smile touched her lips. When she looked back, our eyes met. She looked away quickly, fixing her attention on the food she was preparing, her thoughts private.

'Frank was asking for you.'

'How is he?'

'He's fine, thank God. Enjoying the good weather. Do you remember Peg Larkin?'

'Is that Jimmy Larkin's mother?'

'Yeah. That's right. Didn't you go to school with Jimmy?'

'He was a year ahead of me.'

'Well anyway, the poor woman died last week. She was down in Murphy's on Saturday getting her lotto numbers and she started complaining about a pain in her chest. By the time the ambulance got there she was dead.' She paused, the butter dish in her hand, hovering inches above the table. 'She was the last of the Larkins. There was a whole gang of them in it. My father used to say that Dan Larkin was trying to start his own football team. They all died young, God rest them.'

I had moved away from Wexford to avoid the common-place, but I suffered the same fate as every expatriate. Each visit brings with it a list. Litany. Births, deaths and marriages. You can never get away.

'Are you sure this will be enough?' she said, spreading butter on a slice of bread. 'I could make an omelette or something . . .'

'No, Mother. The sandwiches will be grand.'

She seemed to have grown frail since the funeral, moving

68

around the kitchen gingerly, with the solemn caution of the elderly. The preparation of the snack was a ritual, each task performed with the slow certainty and quiet concentration of something that should be easily familiar but is strangely surreal. Her body had betrayed her, giving in to the outrageous demands of age without so much as a whimper. *Old woman.* It taunted her, protesting when she bent to retrieve a milk carton from the refrigerator. She looked like someone who had to search for a reason to get out of bed in the mornings. I had no doubt that there were days when she didn't find one. Her clothes looked as if she had slept in them, her hair needed washing. *Oh, Mother, why have you let yourself go?*

It was an effort to lift the teapot. She refilled her own mug and poured a cup for me. I always associate the taste of tea with Ireland. Visit someone in Germany and they offer you a beer. 'You'll have a cup of tea,' is a statement in Ireland, not a question.

'So what brings you home, Michael?'

'I came to see you.'

She looked at me, dubious. 'Oh. That's nice.' I thought I caught a trace of sarcasm in her voice. 'You shouldn't be wasting your money, though.'

'I'd hardly call it waste now, Mother.'

She smiled. 'Oh well, it's good to see you anyway.' She sipped her tea. 'How's Maria?'

'Fine . . . She's . . . Fine.'

She put her mug on the table in front of her and looked at me evenly. 'What's wrong, Michael?'

'Nothing. There's nothing wrong.'

'Come on, Michael. I always know when there's something wrong with you. You should know by now that you can't fool me.'

I suppose that is why I had come home. Back to the nest to lick my wounds. I looked out the window. A robin red-breast, perching on her bird-table, seemed to be staring back at me. I didn't want to look at her. I hadn't been there when she needed me. I felt suddenly ashamed for having brought my problems home to her.

'Tell me, Michael.'

'She's gone.'

'Where?'

'I think she's living with her mother. Dublin . . . I don't know. We didn't part on the best of terms.'

'It'll all work out,' she said. 'Lovers' quarrel. That's all.'

My eyes filled with tears. I brushed at them, trying to control myself. 'I'm afraid there's more.' I was crying, tears streaming down my face, my nose running. Child.

She handed me some kitchen roll and reached across the table for my hand. 'It's all right, Michael. Just tell me.'

'I wish . . . Oh Christ.'

'What is it, Michael?'

'I don't know how to tell you this, Mother. There's no easy way to tell you, so I'll just say it. She's going to have a baby.'

She was silent for a moment, her hand stiffening on mine. I couldn't lift my eyes from the floor. I just sat there, sniffing back snot and feeling miserable.

'Oh Jesus Christ.' Shocked. It was almost a sigh. As if the words had just hitched a lift on a passing breath. 'This is a first,' she said, drawing herself together, 'I'm at a loss for words.'

'I'm sorry.' I did not want to look at her, afraid of her reaction. She squeezed my hand.

'It's all right, Michael. There's no need to apologise to me. What about Maria? Why did she come back to Ireland?'

I lifted a tear-streaked face to her. 'I fucked up, Mammy.' She flinched at the language, the venom in my voice. 'I really fucked up.'

Coming around the table, she caught my head in her hands and cradled it against her chest. 'Poor Michael. What are we going to do with you?'

70

I sat sobbing, my neck arched, hands folded in my lap, her hand stroking my cheek as she kissed the top of my head. 'Shush now. There, there.' A sick child, comforted by Mammy, I was eight years old again.

Dublin. Night. Temple Bar. New to me. Rain glistens on the cobblestones. Corybantic crowds congregate wherever there is drink served. We didn't have anything like this when I lived here. Marauders, we invaded old men's pubs. Rowdy children, watched solemnly by seasoned drinkers with bushy white eyebrows and Guinness moustaches. But Dublin is a young man's town now. It has changed, moved along without me. It has passed me by.

*Listen to me. Old fart before my time.* I shuffle along, coat wrapped tight around me, hands sunk deep in pockets against the summer drizzle. A pub door opens to my right. Explosion. Sound, warmth, the smell of drink. A couple spill out onto the street, arms around each other, all smiling faces, teeth and tans. There must be room for me now. I catch the door before it swings shut and force my way into the heaving crowd.

'Gerry? Hi. It's Michael. Fancy a few scoops?' I turn my back to the wall of sound, screw a finger further into my free ear and strain to hear his reply. 'What? I can't hear you. There's a fair bit of crack going on here. Get your arse in gear and get in here. Your pint will be waiting for you.' I can't hear a word he is saying. Maybe he'll come, maybe he won't. I scream the address of the pub into the telephone, hang up and push my way back to the bar.

I went to school with Gerry Hart. He is the only friend that I have from those days. Strange. *Friend.* I use the word loosely. I'm not really sure that he likes me. We did not get on well together at school. Nobody got on well with Gerry. He was a quiet child. Studious. He kept to himself, speaking rarely and bothering nobody. Until, one day, some fuckwit decided that it would be fun to say he was *queer.* For two years Gerry's desk was pushed a few feet from the rest of the class. He would find sandwiches squashed between the pages of his textbooks. He was labelled. Notes stuck to his back. *Kick me, I'm a faggot.* A new cut or bruise would appear almost every day. We knew that it was wrong, but we were afraid. Queers have lovers. *Are you pufter Hart's bum chum, Dwyer?* Moral dilemma in the school gymnasium. I am not a hero. *Of course not. I hate the bastard.* I watch them piss on him in the showers. Although I never joined in the physical abuse, I am sure that I contributed in no small way to the mental cruelty by terminating our budding friendship without a word of explanation. I simply pretended that he did not exist and left him to the vultures.

Gerry is married now with three small children. Not that it matters.

I met him again a couple of years after we left school. He turned up on my doorstep one day, apologetic. His mother had asked mine for my address. 'Just for a couple of days. Sorry. I'm starting an AnCo course tomorrow. I'll kip on the couch.' But we enjoyed each other's company. Easy. Neither of us made demands. We ended up sharing an assortment of flats together for more than two years. He never mentioned our schooldays. I didn't want to broach the subject. After a while an unspoken agreement materialised. Taboo subject. It never happened.

His beer was waiting for him when he arrived. He stood at the door for a minute, his glasses fogging up as he squinted into the crowd, eventually catching sight of me waving him over. He had to shout to be heard as he elbowed his way to the bar. 'Thanks, Dwyer. Jaysus, it's a fuckin' awful night.' He was soaked, his mousey hair stuck to his forehead, water dripping off his nose. He sipped his beer, glancing around the room over the rim of the glass. 'This place is fuckin' jammed.'

'Always the master of the understatement, Hart. How the hell are you?' I punched his shoulder, causing him to slop his drink down his chin.

'You fucker, Dwyer,' he said, wiping at the beer with his already sodden sleeve. 'You're still a bollox, I see.'

'Some things will never change.'

'I suppose not. I'm not too bad actually. Eileen will

probably kill me when she gets me home, but right now I'm grand. How about yourself?'

'Never been better, you old horse's arse.'

'So. What brings you to these parts?'

'Ah, I'm just home for a quick visit.'

He looked at me knowingly. 'Dwyer, you never do anything for the sake of it.' He handed me his beer, took off his trench-coat and dropped it on the ground, a wet heap between him and the bar. 'What's up?'

'Ah, forget it. Let's just say I'm homesick. I am in serious need of a few beers and a bit of crack. Have you spotted the talent in here?'

'Of course not,' he grinned at me. 'I'm a happily married man.'

'Go 'way, you lech. You're not blind. Do you see that blonde over there? I was talking to her earlier. Scottish. Great personality.'

'I can see that.'

'Aye. And there's an American at the other side of the bar that I'm seriously thinking of shagging. You see her? She's a New Zealander. We were contemplating setting up a sheep farm together just before you arrived. In fact, I do believe we're the only Irish people in the place.'

'Could be.'

'You know what they say. Everybody has a little bit of Irish in them. If not, I'm prepared to help out.'

'Well it'd be a very fuckin' small piece then, Dwyer.'

'Jealousy, my friend. An ugly thing. By the way, it's your round.'

We ended up at his house at two o' clock in the morning. The queue for the taxi had been a pantomime. A gentleman with a bleeding ear, wishing to share the cost of a taxi to Finglas, had arrived half an hour after we joined the queue. He jumped into every taxi that came along, drunkenly beseeching the rightful occupants to take him home. 'I've money,' he would slur, proffering a pocketful of pound coins.

Eventually he would be hauled onto the street by an apprentice body-builder who was next to us in the queue. When our turn came he asked if he could join us. I answered in German. He paused, looked at me blankly for about ten seconds, then jumped into the front seat.

'For Jaysus sake,' roared his tormentor. He stamped up to the taxi, pulled the door open, dragged the poor unfortunate into the street, and started to beat the living daylights out of him. The taxi driver didn't bat an eyelid.

'Where to, lads?'

'Clontarf. Right beside the castle.'

We drove off, the two of us looking out the back window as the muscle man began dunking the guy from Finglas in the 'Floozy in the Jacuzzi'. Gerry looked at me.

'What?' I said.

'We could have given him a lift, you know.'

'You're soft, Hart.'

Eileen didn't give him a hard time at all. She was watching a video when we arrived. She embraced me warmly and told us to sit by the fire while she made us a cup of coffee. She sat with us for a little while, making small-talk. When she asked how Maria was I made a non-committal answer and changed the subject. She took the hint and let it pass. After a few minutes she excused herself and went to bed, leaving us to our own devices. Gerry retrieved a bottle of brandy from somewhere and poured some into our coffees.

'Have you given up the smokes?' I asked.

'Jesus, don't talk to me. I've been off them for a month. It's killin' me.' He sat back in an armchair at the other side of the grate.

'Eileen too?'

'Yeah. We're like bears with sore heads. Always snapping at each other. This is the sort of thing divorce was invented for.' I smiled weakly into the fire. He seemed to sense the change in me. 'So, how is Maria?'

75

'Like I said. Grand.'

'Michael, the last time we spent a night in a pub eyeing up the talent wasn't today or yesterday. Are you two okay?' I swirled the coffee and brandy around in the bottom of the mug and stared into the fire. He sighed. 'Well. It's obvious you're not okay,' he said. 'How bad is it?'

'Pretty bad, Gerry. To the point that it's not an issue any more.'

'Oh shit.'

'Yeah. Oh shit. I'm afraid I'm a bachelor again, Gerry.' I smiled at him. 'God help the female population, huh?'

He looked stunned. 'Jesus, Michael.' He spoke slowly, shaking his head. 'I'm really sorry. What happened?'

'Suffice it to say, there's a baby involved.'

'Oh sweet Christ. Is she going to keep it?'

'I think so. We're not exactly on speaking terms. She moved home. That's why I'm here. I want to try to see her.'

'Christ, Michael. I'm shocked. I . . . I don't know what to say really.' He was staring into the cup in his hands. Suddenly he shivered, as if something cold had been touched against his spine. He looked up at me. 'How long has all this been going on? I mean, when did she leave?'

'About two weeks ago.'

He shook his head again. 'Michael. If you don't mind me asking . . . Why? I mean . . . Did you not want the baby or something?'

I looked steadily at him. 'Do you remember Claire Roche?'

His mouth dropped open. 'Oh no. Michael. You didn't.'

'I'm afraid I did.'

He laughed, uneasy, sat back, crossed his legs and contemplated me for a long moment.

'You fucking gobshite, Dwyer.'

'Thanks, mate. I knew you'd understand.'

He ran a hand down his face, stretching the skin, his

lower lip curling over his puckered chin. 'Apart from anything else, I lose.'

'What?'

'Eileen said you'd never settle down. We had a bet. She reckoned you were the proverbial leopard.'

I smiled humourlessly across the room at him. Leopard. Cheetah. Cheater. I looked away.

The room brought back memories. This was where Maria met Gerry and Eileen for the first time. The same day we all got drunk together for the first time. The same day that I met Maria's mother. A long weekend of meetings. New friends, new foes. Sometime during the evening Maria and Eileen became best friends while Gerry and I became inebriated. Bacardi bonding. Eileen never trusted me. With good reason it turns out. Over the years her friendship with Maria made the situation worse. She tolerated me for Gerry's sake but loathed me for what she knew I was capable of doing to Maria. She cornered me at a disco in Frankfurt during one of their visits, asking me out for a slow set. She put her arms around my neck, snuggled close to me, smiled and looked up into my face, lips parted slightly. Pulling my head down, she got close to my ear and said, 'I know what you are, even if Gerry and Maria don't. You're an evil, egocentric bastard, and if you hurt either one of them I'll chop your balls off.' She leaned back, smiling sweetly, eyes soft with alcohol, reached down and twisted my left testicle. Then she turned on her heel, leaving me gasping with pain in the middle of the crowded dance floor. Next morning she appeared at the breakfast table bright and breezy, making me wonder if I had dreamed the whole incident.

Gerry leaned over and poured some more brandy into my mug. I could see the top of his head, hair thinning, sunburned bald patch. 'Jesus,' I thought, 'none of us are getting any younger.' I felt suddenly old. Deflated. I lifted the rim of my mug against the bottle. 'Thanks.' *I remembered him, stubborn child, cold in the corner of the shower room, soaked*

77

*in urine, tears welling in his eyes. Burning eyes. He would not cry. Defiant.* 'Gerry. I'm sorry.'

'For what?'

'All of it. Everything.'

He looked at me, quizzical. 'I think you're drunk, Dwyer.'

I smiled sadly. The fire cracked. A spark, bright orange comet, arched its way across the grate and plunged into the pockmarked carpet. Sinking. Drowning. Black. Acrid smell. He didn't notice one more smoking crater beside his left knee, oblivious, me the centre of his attention. Poised, bottle still angled towards me in his outstretched hand, he looked into my face, every feature open, unguarded. A study of concern for a friend. Quiet, confident. This man. This children's casualty. Walking wounded. He, of all men, should be a simpering wreck. Should be the simpering wreck that I have visualised. *I've been feeling sorry for you all these years.* Look at you. Oak. Straight. Strong. How? I should be the Gregory Peck. I am the hero. Quintessential leading man.

'Don't the bastards ever get to you?'

He said nothing. Worried wrinkles marched across his face and gathered at his forehead.

'Gerry. How can you be so, I don't know, content? Why don't you stand in the street and howl at the moon?'

He stood up, right knee popping, eyes still fixed on me, and placed the bottle carefully on the mantelpiece. 'Is that how you feel, Michael? Like howling at the moon?'

'Yes. No. Sometimes. I don't know.' I could feel myself losing control, could feel the frustration building in me.

He squatted in front of me, right hand resting lightly on my forearm. 'Michael. Forgive me. We've been friends a long time. Apart from the baby. Apart from the ruined romance. Apart from too much to drink tonight. Apart from all that. What the fuck is your problem?' He grinned up at me and squeezed my arm, then settled back into his chair. I couldn't help myself. I grinned back at him and wiped my hands across my face. I sniffed, coughed, and tried to regain my composure.

'Christ, Gerry. Isn't that enough?' My voice was thick with emotion, words squeezed through tight throat.

'Come on, Michael. Pull yourself together. I've never seen you like this. To tell you the truth, it's not a very pretty sight.'

'I'm . . . My whole life is turning to shite, Gerry. I don't know what I'm doing any more.'

He snorted. 'Welcome to the human race.'

'No. Seriously. I thought I had it all under control. Good job, loads of money, nice car, no real commitments. Fuck. I have it all.' I looked at him through teary eyes. 'So why am I so damned miserable?'

'You tell me.'

'I don't know, Gerry. I just don't know. What am I doing wrong?'

He sighed and leaned forward, scratching the back of his neck. 'Michael, I could give you a whole set of answers. But they'd be my answers. You're going to have to work it out for yourself, mate.'

I tightened my grip on my coffee cup, kneading it. 'I love her, Gerry. I really do.' I was staring into the fireplace.

'Oh, for fuck's sake.' His voice had changed suddenly, hardened, forcing my head to snap around, my eyes to lock on his. 'Cop yourself on, Michael. You don't love anyone but yourself. You never have. If you love her so much, what the fuck were you doing bonking Claire Roche?' That hurt. I felt my eyes melt away from his. He was suddenly consumed by anger. 'You'd want to start sorting yourself out, boy. Who do you think you are? Peter fucking Pan? Grow up, man. Sometimes I think you're incapable of having an adult conversation, let alone a real friendship.'

'What about us?' I was on the defensive now. 'We've been friends for years.'

'No, Michael. I've been friends for years.' He stood up. 'Face the facts. When was the last time you picked up the phone to call me just to see how I was? You've been in Germany for what? Five or six years? How many letters did you write? One? "Here's my address . . . Write to me." I've called you at least once a month. I've sent you birthday cards, Christmas cards, letters, photos of the kids. Jesus, Michael. You turn up here once or twice a year, like a movie star or something, and expect everyone to drop everything and bow down and adore. Lord fuckin' Muck. Maria is one terrific lady, Michael. If you have any sense you'll stop feeling sorry for yourself and go crawling back on your hands and knees. Jesus. You really are a self-absorbed, morally indigent, arrogant git.'

Gerry had never raised his voice to me before. He was standing over me, fists clenched, eyes flashing. I sat, stunned, looking up at him. He put a hand to his forehead, closing his eyes, trying to control himself.

'Sorry, Michael. It's none of my business really. Damn it, though. Sometimes I get so mad at you.' I had never noticed. 'I'm going to bed before I wake the kids up. You're in the usual room. Eileen moved Paul in with Helen and Patricia.'

Then he was gone, leaving me alone beside the fire.

He appeared for breakfast the next morning somewhat the worse for wear, unshaven, his hair tossed. His eyes were like piss-holes in snow. *The children had erupted into my room at seven o'clock, informed, no doubt, by Mammy that 'Uncle Michael' would be delighted to see them.* He crossed the room gingerly, like a man walking on eggshells, rubbing at his tired face and carefully avoiding my eye. Eileen put a cup of tea in front of him as soon as he settled at the head of the table. He muttered his thanks and glanced at me. An embarrassed smile crept onto his lips.

'Sorry about last night, mate. I think I must have had too much to drink.'

'Don't be sorry. You were right.' Words. Easy.

'No. I was way out of line. Sorry.'

'Forget it.'

We had breakfast together, Gerry, his wife, his children and me. I sat among them, laughing, playing with the children, cutting up sausages for the youngest. I caught Eileen looking at me several times during the meal, as if trying to make up her mind what she wanted to say to me. After breakfast, Gerry took the children into the living-room to watch a Postman Pat video. I stayed sitting at the table with Eileen.

'Gerry told me,' she said.

'I guessed.'

'We never got on that well, Michael, and I don't know if my advice is welcome, but I'm going to give it to you just the same.' She sipped her tea, elbows propped on the table, mug held in both hands.

'I could do with some advice,' I said.

'Like I said, we never got on that well. But my kids love you. They can't wait for you to come. They hate when you leave. You're good with them, Michael. You'd make a good father if you could keep your zipper fastened. Go make up with Maria. Marry her, have the baby, and buy yourself a chastity belt. That's the only way you're ever going to be happy.'

I smiled into my mug. 'You're probably right.'

'You know I'm right. You're not stupid, Michael. You just pretend you are.' She smiled across the table at me. It felt as though we almost liked each other, sitting at her table, smiling at each other as the early morning sun streamed through the window. Gerry came back into the kitchen, singing the praises of Postman Pat, the babysitter. Eileen refilled our mugs. The children's laughter floated down the hall. I felt peaceful, happy, surrounded by this family. I drank my tea, accepted another slice of toast and marmalade, and talked to my friends.

A clock ticked loudly on the mantelpiece. Her mother sat silently on the sofa, never taking her eyes off me. Hawk. Knees together, back straight. Cold, blue, piercing eyes. Cruel mouth curled, mocking, white lips tight together, hiding harmful words. She didn't have to speak. I knew what she thought of me the moment she opened the door, the way her face hardened. Granite. She watched me, unblinking, like some giant reptile, as I sat in her Laura Ashley living-room, waiting for the daughter I had desecrated.

I cleared my throat, as if to speak. She raised an eyebrow, daring me. *Just try it.* I sat back, crossed my legs, and looked around me. She stayed with me to make sure I didn't touch anything, filthy fingers having done enough damage. Would she sterilise this seat when I left?

Maria arrived, looking tired. There were black circles beneath her eyes. She looked pale. Her mother stood and walked stiffly towards the door. 'I'll be in the kitchen,' she said to Maria as she passed. She threw a final, scornful look at me before she closed the door.

Maria stood awkwardly behind an armchair, as if needing its protection, keeping it between us. *Isn't there already enough between us?*

'How are you, Maria?'

'Okay.' She smiled, a tiny reflex smile. One corner of her mouth twitched, a muscle in her cheek flexed and gathered, then released. 'What do you want, Michael?'

'I came to apologise.'

'So apologise and leave me alone.'

I sighed, looking away from her. The clock ticked. I heard her shift her weight, her clothes rustling, a soft breath exhaled.

'Look, Maria. This isn't easy for me either.'

'Good.' Tight word. Snapped out, like a rubber band breaking.

I ignored her. 'The truth is, I really am sorry. Can't we at least try to be friends? Take it from there? For the sake of the baby.'

She laughed, a sort of snort of derision. 'Friends? Michael, you should know I'm choosy about my friends.'

'What about the baby?'

'What *about* the baby?' She leaned towards me, her voice hard. Eyes wide, whites showing, as if daring me. 'What on earth do you think you can give it that I can't? Teach it to lie? To play with people's emotions? I think, for the sake of the baby, the best thing you can do, Michael, is fuck right off.'

She stood behind her armchair, nostrils flared, head thrust forward, little feet apart, hands clawing at the headrest.

'I didn't mean to hurt you, Maria.'

'No, Michael. You never mean anything, do you? The truth is you were just doing what suited you. I just happened to be in the way.'

'Maria, I'm sorry.'

'Oh, shut up, Michael. You're sorry for yourself. You want me to ease your conscience, don't you?'

'No.'

'Then why did you come here?'

I stood looking at her for a moment before replying. 'I don't know,' I said tiredly.

But I did know. I am a greedy man. Never let go of anything in case you miss something. I wanted Maria. I wanted the baby. But I wanted more. I wanted Claire. I wanted my freedom. I want. I want. I want. I am a child in a sweet shop, my eyes are bigger than my belly. I want it all.

'What makes you think I'm going to make things easy for you, Michael?' She screwed her face up, as if tasting something sour.

'I don't want you to make things easy for me. I just want to talk, okay?'

'Okay. Talk.' She folded her arms.

I stood up and fingered a candlestick on the mantelpiece, my back to her. I imagined her mother, carefully wiping everything I might have touched with a damp cloth when I was gone. 'After you left, I started thinking.' I spoke slowly, careful measured words. 'Maybe the baby is the best thing that could have happened. Maybe it will bring us back together.'

'If you can't commit to me without a baby, you won't commit with one. This isn't a game, Michael. I'm not using the baby to try to snare you.' The words were clipped. She was barely controlling her temper.

'I know, I know. That's not what I'm saying. I . . . '

'What, Michael? What are you saying?'

'Give me a break, Maria. This is hard.' Mistake. I shouldn't have snapped at her.

'Yes, Michael. It is.' Her voice had tightened another notch.

'Look. All I'm saying is that we can't just . . . I don't know . . . pretend nothing has happened between us.'

'You're right, Michael. I can't pretend nothing has happened. Do you think I'm a total fucking imbecile?'

'What do you mean?'

'You know full well.'

Claire. We had never mentioned it. We had avoided the subject in our fights. I had never been sure, but I had suspected that she knew. She let me wander, gave me time and space, waited for me to come back to her. She never asked me, never challenged me. Confronting this thing would have spelled the end for us and that was more than she could bear. I didn't know what to say. Suddenly everything seemed final. Words became meaningless. 'I'm sorry, Maria.'

She looked at me, unimpressed. I was something unsavoury, not to be stepped in. Suddenly the fight seemed to ebb out of her. Her face softened. Her shoulders drooped. She looked tired and small again. Beaten.

'Okay, Michael. Friends. Okay? We're buddies. You have nothing to be sorry for. Now fuck off and leave me alone.'

I took a step towards her, but she raised a hand, palm outwards, stopping me in mid-step. 'Don't touch me.' Her face was angled away from me, her features screwed up, eyes closed, as if the very thought of my touch made her feel ill. I just stood there, in the middle of the room, hovering, twisting my jacket in my hands, searching for something to say. She didn't move. Arm still extended, shoulders set against me, pained expression. The clock ticked. Time ran out. When she spoke again, it was in a tiny, little girl voice. 'Just go, Michael. Please.'

I hesitated. Opened my mouth. Closed it. I could see a tear squeeze its way from behind her eyelid and run down the side of her nose. Her chin puckered and began to tremble. I moved towards her, past her, and through the doorway. Her mother came out of the kitchen, rosary beads wrapped around her right hand, as I made my way to the front door. She traced my progress, wordless, disapproving. I did not acknowledge her. My eyes brushed across her brown shoes, support stockings, green skirt, the hem of her grey cardigan. They alighted for a moment on her hands, joined as if in prayer. Gold wedding band, red beads. I could feel her hatred as I passed her in the hallway. *I cast you from this place, evil spirit.* I opened the front door. Air. Sunshine. Traffic. Noise. People. A number ten bus roared past. I stepped into the street and closed the door behind me.

An ocean of sound engulfed me, buffeted me. After the stifling silence of her living-room, the noise and motion made my head spin. Unreal. I walked up the North Circular Road, towards the Phoenix Park. People stood at bus stops, cars raced by, children laughed, old ladies gossiped. Strange. I quickened my pace. Birds sang, sunlight baked hot concrete, tar boiled and bubbled on the road. Stranger. I began to run. Nobody took any notice. Wild man running up the North Circular Road. I sprinted. Effortless. Faster. Faster. Trees rushed past. An old man hobbled by at speed. A dog barked in a garden. A girl on a bicycle crawled backwards and fell behind me. It felt as though I was stationary, the world was moving, and I was a stranger. Observing. Watching. It didn't make any difference what I did, what I said. I was a stranger in this world. Her world.

I stopped and gulped back great lungfulls of air. My heart pounded. My head throbbed. I steadied myself against the gate to the Phoenix Park and squatted down, squinting into the sunlight. 'Oh Jesus.' I thought. Then, aloud, I said, 'Jesus. Fuck. Bollox. Christ.' A woman, walking past with a small child, tut-tutted and gave me a wide berth. I put my head in my hands, my elbows resting on my knees, and squeezed my temples, then raked my fingers down my face. I stayed like that for a few minutes, on my haunches, watching the traffic, women pushing prams, feeling the sweat run down my forehead and drip onto my forearms. 'If she doesn't want me, she doesn't want me,' I thought. I transferred all the blame to her, just like that. *I tried. I made the effort. Her fault.* I was blameless. Shameless.

I looked down the hill. A bus was pulling in to the bus stop. I stood up, walked towards it, and climbed aboard. When we passed the house, I looked at its green door and lifeless windows. I pictured her being comforted in the living room by her harpy mother. *You're better off without him. Praise the Lord.* I could see her face, all tears and runny nose. I remembered her slumped in our hallway. My hallway. I thought of her packing her suitcase quietly in that hotel room. *Could you go out for a few minutes, please?* I saw her in the Shamrock, dropping her bombshell. *I'm late!* Too late.

The bus rumbled past. I continued to look at the house as we trundled towards St Peter's Church. Greedy me. I never want to let go. I let go.

# DAILY BREAD

I miss Saturday afternoons with you, Maria. Early days. Exploration. Learning about each other. Learning about Germany. Learning to survive. You hated how the shops closed here. 'If we were in Dublin now we could go shopping on Grafton Street.' But Germany becomes a giant ghost town on Saturday afternoons. Closed for the weekend. Everybody hides. Imaginary tumbleweed, camouflaged in dust clouds, swirls victorious down the deserted *Zeil*. Past *Hauptwache*, Brazilian buskers play to gnarly knots of people, hunched against the cold. 'Let's go to France,' you say. 'Because we can. Or Luxembourg.'

Day trips. We have escaped from the island. Eyes wide with wonder, we flee across borders. Migrant forays, flights of fancy. Strasbourg is just a step away. And Sunday, all quiet on the Frankfurt front, we sit together examining our prizes. Champagne and *foie gras*, with toast made from Marks and Spencer's sliced pan. We are children on Christmas morning, marshmallow misty, dipping into daydreams.

So many things I miss about Saturday afternoons with you.

Claire? You'd like her. She's nice.

But I've done it all before. Nothing to discover now. We have seen castles on the Rhine, majestic, and driven underneath the Alps. We have crossed the Gothard Pass in June, and thrown snowballs at each other in the clouds. Saturday afternoons with you, each one a new adventure.

With her, Saturday afternoons, sometimes we fuck.

'So he's gone for, like, half an hour at this stage,' Dave was in full flow when I walked into the Shamrock. He saw me squinting into the depths of the bar and raised a red paw. 'Mick, how are ya?'

I wandered towards them. 'Dave, Simon, Joe. How's it goin'?'

Nods all round. Voices. Welcome. *Howaya, Michael? Mick.*

Dave was all smiles. 'I was just tellin' the lads about McDonald. You're not going to believe this, but I swear it's true.'

'Go on,' I pulled up a barstool, threw my jacket over it, and sat down. A barman shuffled over and looked at me expectantly. 'Guinness.'

'Right,' Dave got back into gear. 'The story so far. We get a contract for a system in Brussels, okay? Myself and McDonald volunteer to drive the stuff over from Dublin last weekend. Free trip to Dublin first. You know the way.' I nodded. 'We're on the ferry, right? Stocious. We've been knockin' 'em back since Rosslare. So McDonald fucks off to the jacks. I'm sittin' there half an hour later. No sign of his nibs. So I decide to go and look for him.' Dave looked as if he could barely contain himself. 'You'll never guess where I found him.'

My Guinness arrived, cloudy and headless. You get used to it. 'With a wench, no doubt. Some young one's cabin?' Dave just grinned at me. I grinned back. 'Okay. So where did you find him?'

'I get back to the cabin and I hear this frightened little voice goin', "Help. Help." McDonald's on the loo. Stuck fast, with his trousers round his ankles and this big red face. It turns out that he pushed the flush button while he was still sittin' on the loo and got sucked in.'

This was greeted with hoots of laughter.

'Stupid fuckin' gobshite,' said Joe.

Simon struggled to control himself. 'What did you do?'

'What could I do?' Dave said, the picture of wide-eyed

innocence. 'I went to get a stewardess.'

'Bastard!' Three voices in unison.

'So she comes in, not a bother on her, and sez, "You've created a vacuum, sir. I'm afraid the only way out is to break wind."'

'Fart?' asked Joe, incredulous.

'Who says flatulence will get you nowhere?' said Simon.

'Oh well, Jesus,' I took a sip from my pint. 'No bother there. McDonald's speciality, the smelly fucker. He could fart Dixie through a keyhole.'

'Could he fuck! A man famous for flatulence on three continents, and he couldn't get one out. Apparently he was too embarrassed. It took fifteen minutes to work up the wind.'

'Oh, Christ.' The tears were rolling down Simon's cheeks. 'I don't believe a word of it. You're making it up.'

'No. I swear it's true. And he sez to me, you know, "Dave," he sez. "Don't tell anyone, will you?"'

I grinned at him. 'And of course you promised not to breathe a word.'

'Of course.' He held a hand over his heart and tried to look offended. 'Would I ever talk about such a personal misfortune?' He paused for effect. 'Not half, wouldn't I.'

We all laughed again, shaking our heads and muttering. *Jesus. Gobshite.*

These men were my peers. My friends. Men that I had little in common with, except my exile. Thrown together, we were chameleons, fused, developing a single personality. We talked about each other and the common enemy, the Germans. We talked about how much we hated being here. I craved acceptance, acquiring a knowledge of hurling to rival that of any man alive. 'I used to play hurling at school,' I had stated. It would have been more accurate to say that the Christian Brothers had regularly forced me onto the field, hurley in hand, cowering under the flight of ball, praying that play would bypass me. Hurling had seemed to me to be a game where thirty boys were given sticks and told to beat the living shit out of each other for Ireland. But my interest had germinated since my expatriation. Maria had been constantly subjected to complaints that I could not attend matches. The fact that I never went when I had the chance was irrelevant. I had learned to see the beauty in the game. The speed. The skill.

'How's Maria?' Joe asked.

'Grand.'

'You got a visa for the night, then?'

'Yeah, something like that.' Why should I bother telling him?

The pub was dark and crowded. The smoke stung my eyes. It seemed that, as usual, the clientele was an amalgam, one part Irish, one part German and ninety-eight parts American soldier. The Killarney Kid, wearing a large cowboy hat and introducing songs in a Californian accent, stood on a small stage. Serial killer, he murdered Irish ballads. The soldiers lapped it up.

My bladder decided it was time for an empty. I slipped off my barstool and touched Dave's elbow. 'Arnold.'

'What?'

'I'll be back.'

The stench of urine was overpowering in the gents. An American was leaning against the wall, his head against one oversized forearm, trying to coax a performance from an uncooperative assistant. He was listing heavily to starboard and I stood in front of the next urinal praying, for my shoes' sake, that he would be unsuccessful for another couple of minutes. He looked at me with far from focused eyes and grinned, 'Jesus, man, don't ya fuckin' hate it when ya can't piss?'

I looked at him. 'Yeah. Bummer.'

'Hey man, where ya from?'

'Ireland.'

'No shit?'

'Yeah.' I went to the sink to wash my hands. He moved away from the urinal and stood in front of me. I noticed that he had forgotten to put his penis away.

He put a hand on my shoulder, 'God damn, man. My grandmother is Irish.'

His breath was making me dizzy. I looked around for something clean to dry my hands with. I gave up and used my tee-shirt. 'Cool. Listen, I'll see you round.' I started for the door.

'Hey, I gotta buy you a beer.'

'Some other time, okay?' I tried to walk around him.

'I'm tryin' to be friendly here, man.'

There was something dangerous in his voice. I paused and looked at him evenly, considering. 'Sure. Why not? But zip your fly up first. Okay?'

We returned to the lounge where I discovered that every American soldier in the place had an Aunty May from Donegal that I was sure to know. It seemed that a genuine Irishman was a rarity in this particular Irish pub. I shook hands with everybody, drank my beer, made my excuses, and hurried back to Dave, Simon and Joe at the bar.

'It appears that I've been elected Irish ambassador for the evening.' I said. 'What are you lot laughing at?'

'You pick 'em, don't you?' grinned Simon.

I threw him a filthy look. 'I knew he was drunk. His face was blurred.'

'Everyone's an Irishman at heart, eh?' said Joe as four pints of Guinness arrived in front of us, courtesy of my new found friends. We raised our glasses to them across the lounge.

'Gobshites,' I spat. 'Fucking nomads.'

'Oh Jesus,' moaned Simon. 'Here we go again.'

'Seriously,' I turned to him. 'The only reason these fuckers are here is because they can't hack it in their own country.'

'And why are we here, Mick?' Simon looked amused.

'Because we choose to be,' I answered. 'We have great jobs. We're raking in the money. Earning more than we could ever do at home. We're not threatened with the dole queue every time we fuck up. We're the crème de la crème, boys. Or hadn't you noticed?'

'Speak for yourself,' said Simon.

'These guys are soldiers, for fuck's sake. Soldiers. They're on a tour of duty. It's like a prison sentence. In some cases it's instead of a prison sentence. All they ever talk about is "when I get back stateside this" and "when I get back stateside that". They have their own shops. Their cars even have American number plates. They have their own rules and regulations and live in their own little self-sufficient villages where they pay homage to the "Land of the Free" and play baseball every Sunday afternoon. Bollox.'

Simon smiled. 'How many pounds of Irish sausages do you have in the freezer, Michael?'

Dave winked at me. 'Personally, I've always thought that having one Irish sausage was enough.'

I ignored the laughter, ignored Dave grabbing at his crotch. 'Listen. To them America is a bright light that they've been staring at for too long. They have their eyes closed now. They're worshipping its afterimage.'

'So?'

'They meet a fucking Irishman and all of a sudden they all come from Bally-go-backwards. Next thing you know a Scotsman'll walk in and they'll all break into the highland fling and start calling each other Angus. It's enough to make you sick. A whole fucking nation without a personality. They're all so busy searching for their roots they can't settle for what they've got. They keep looking over their shoulders and wishing their lives away, trying to claim everybody else's heritage. One of these days they'll wake up and discover that they forgot to build one of their own. Gobshites.'

Simon looked at me over his glasses. 'Live and let live, Mick.'

'I'm just sick of the bastards. I wish they'd all just fuck off back to America and leave us alone.'

'I don't know what you're getting so excited about. They're in here every night of the week.'

'I know. In an Irish pub. That's exactly the point.'

'What point?' Simon was ready for an argument. 'You're not exactly making a lot of sense, Michael, *a chara*.' I stood, finger raised, face flushed. Suddenly I realised the stupidity of it. I looked at this bespectacled buffoon in front of me. Stage Irishman. Idiot. I looked around me. Idiots, all of them. It dawned on me. I didn't actually like a single one of them.

'I don't know which is worse,' I muttered, to nobody in particular. 'A group of American soldiers, drinking themselves stupid in an Irish pub in Frankfurt, or us. We are fucking pathetic. An Irish pub, for fuck's sake. In Frankfurt. Pretending we're at home. Pretending this is normal. I don't want to be a part of this any more.'

I put the putrid pint of Guinness on the bar, picked up my jacket, and started to walk away.

'Are you off, Dwyer?' Simon seemed surprised. 'What about your pint?'

I stopped and looked at him. 'Fuck it. It tastes like piss anyway. If you want it you can have it.'

'Thanks.'

And he would drink it too. No pride. Somewhere along the way we all lost our pride. Sapped by the uncertainty that comes from severing your roots. We became hybrids, freaks, neither one thing nor the other. *Paddy, fucking, play-to-the-gallery*. Enough.

When I got outside it was raining. A soft, damp drizzle that reminded me of Ireland. The hum of the pub followed me into the street, the Killarney Kid was singing 'Galway Bay'. I put my jacket on, buried my face in my hands, and rubbed hard at my eyes. I felt suddenly tired, drained. 'What the fuck are you doing, Dwyer?'

I whispered to myself. 'You should go back. Have your pint.'

But I knew that I would not go back. Another tie severed. A false bond broken. I had seen the truth for just a moment, and that was enough. I did not belong with those people, I was not one of them. *Michael Dwyer, proud man. Time to find some dignity.* Even if it is alone. I stepped out into Sachsenhausen.

The rain formed a fine film on my clothes and hair. I turned my jacket collar up and stuck my hands into my pockets. Water trickled down the sides of my face, down my neck, and into my tee-shirt. I stopped and stood under a streetlamp, loud music pumping from a pub behind me, watching people hurry by. All races, creeds and colours. Frankfurt. Melting pot. 'I'm not the only one,' I thought. 'Not the only one running away. I am not the only pilgrim here.'

# II

II

# INTO TEMPTATION

I live in solitary splendour now. Like a lion. Caged. Observed. This is not my natural environment, but I accept it. Noble. Proud. I've made it mine. Footfalls, padding from place to place, there is an air of majesty about me. People stop and stare. I know. I stand out in a crowd. As if a sunbeam follows me. I am never normal. Nothing so mundane. And if I cry, I cry alone. No weakness ever shown. Old scars, white across my hide, are mysteries. Former lives. I am here now. This is me. Captivity. Don't ask me to explain. Guarded thoughts. What made you? I cannot, will not, say.

'Mick, you want a beer?'

'No.' Peasant. Always I refuse. I see them mutter. *Who the fuck does he think he is?* Better than you, you bollox. I have to be. Better than you.

Frankfurt has become like Wexford, home but never home. I find myself walking by the river and thinking about the sea. Buildings stretch, like fingers, pointing somewhere else. But where? I thought I could belong here. I did. For a while. *Auslander.* Look around.

I miss Maria, badly. I miss a lot of things. Sex? There's Claire. She comes here once a month, but that's not it. Maria made me belong.

The days are getting colder. My left shoe lets in water. That's how I know it's raining all the time. Maria would have made me buy a new pair by now. Or bought them for me. They're scuffed. Haven't seen a lick of polish since she left. My hair is long. I only shave on every second day. And people have begun to notice. Looking at me funny. I sit sweating at meetings, centrally heated, wearing heavy jumpers. Another day I climbed out of bed, hungover, too late to iron a shirt for work.

Sometimes I startle myself, sitting in front of the television, farting. *Was that me?* Aloud. 'Who else do you think it was, you fucking moron?'

The sink stands, poised on its predella, waiting. Yesterday's dishes. Or Wednesday's. Whatever. I'll do them tomorrow. Or Wednesday. Beer bottles stand to attention, welcoming me home. Pizza boxes hide behind doorways. Maria. Look what I've done.

*'Are you proud of yourself, Michael?'*

Behind closed doors.

Bachelor. Suits me. Sometimes. But sometimes I feel so alone.

I was born on the twenty-third of December. Extracted, glistening, and proffered to proud parents, like an early Christmas present. A child is born. Two days. All birthdays and Christmases rolled into one. Like angels, they announced their news, triumphant. Angels handing out cigars. *Mother and child are doing well.* Not any more.

Thirty-three today, I'm entering my Jesus year. Alone. I am a child no longer. And adulthood persuades that there are limits to me. Remember Robert ranting about 'youths on motorcycles'? We laughed, Maria. Our old young friend. But now young men with baseball hats give me pause for thought. And if I wear one people stare. Or do I imagine that? Old fart. I am becoming my father, but not the bits about him I preferred.

I chose to be alone today. My mother would have made me welcome. Disappointment dripped along the line when I told her.

*'So you're not coming?'*

*'No.'*

'*Oh!*'

Disembodied, she clung to the connection.

'*I thought a cake maybe . . .* '

First Christmas alone, Mother. I hadn't thought of that. Mine too.

I left work early today. Nobody remembered my birthday. A party, but not for me. Champagne started flowing at three o'clock. An hour later I struggled into my coat, hoisted my briefcase and headed for the door.

'*Tschüs*, Michael. Happy Christmas.' A wet kiss started on my lips and spread across my face, leaving lipstick, like a wound, red, ragged, dragged from the corner of my mouth, splitting my cheek. She caught my hand before it found the door handle, pulling me around. Her eyes were heavy and dull with drink. 'One for the *Strassenbahn*?'

'No, Petra. Thanks. I've got to go.'

'Oh.' She pouted, reluctant to release me. Putting an arm around my neck, she pulled my face down towards her. I could smell the alcohol on her breath. 'Look. We are under the mistletoe, are we not? A Christmas kiss.'

I moved to kiss her cheek, but she turned towards me at the last minute, crushing her lips to mine. I felt her tongue, like a wet worm, wriggle against my teeth. Stepping back, I pushed her away gently. 'I've got to go. See you. Happy Christmas.'

Leaving behind a swirl of party hats and confetti, I shouldered my way through the door and into a freezing fog. Bright blues and reds, laughter, warm bodies, giving way to grey to match my mood. I licked at my lips, tasting her lipstick, sweet on the tip of my tongue. I brushed at my mouth with the back of my hand and walked home, light-headed from too much champagne. My footsteps seemed to echo on the pavement. Children, carrying lanterns, emerged from the fog from time to time, like miniature Jack-the-Rippers, grotesque in colourful clothing, surrounded by bobbing haloes flung from their fairy lights.

When I reached the flat, I poured a whiskey and let my coat fall limp on the floor. I stood in the kitchen, hand on a worktop, glass held, upended, to my lips, and felt the liquid burn my gullet. After refilling the glass, I took the bottle, walked to the living-room and sat with the lights off in the gathering gloom listening to Bach and getting drunk.

'Thirty-three today. Cheers.'

At seven-thirty the phone rang, jerking me from sleep. I sat for a moment in the darkness, wondering where I was. The phone rang again and I reached for it, knocking over the empty whiskey bottle.

'Fuck. Hello.'

'That is not very nice. Hello you too, fuck.' A woman's voice. German.

'Sorry. Who is this?'

'This is Petra. You okay?' It would be a lie to say that I did not know what she wanted. It was obvious. It had been for a long time. Slinking into my office, bending over my desk, one button too many open. A little too much flesh on view. She had never been subtle. I ignored it, knowing. I had my rules. Never with anyone from work.

'Yeah. Sure. Petra. What can I do for you?' My head hurt. I needed to brush my teeth. A fungus had gathered on my tongue.

'You are a naughty boy, aren't you?' She giggled at me.

'What?'

'You didn't tell me your news.' She waited for me to respond.

'I'm sorry, Petra. I've either got a hangover or I'm drunk, I'm not sure which yet, but I haven't got a fucking clue what you're talking about.'

She laughed again. 'Your woman. She is *weg*. She is not here any more. Anka told me at the party.'

'No. She left some time ago.' Office gossip, for once, had been slow.

'Are you a lonely boy?' I could almost see her simpering,

lower lip hung in mock sadness, painted eyelids fluttering. Seductress of sorts. I sighed.

'That depends.'

'Mm. Have you ever had a German woman?' My turn to laugh.

'You're very direct.'

'I know. Many men have told me that. But I am a natural blonde. You know what is said. About blondes. They are having more fun.'

'Is that so?'

'Would you like to find out?'

I paused. 'Like I said. That depends.'

'Do you like games?'

'I haven't hung up yet, have I? What sort of games did you have in mind?' I could feel myself hardening.

'You know. All sorts. We could play.'

'Could we now?'

'Now?' She gasped. Pretending to be shocked. 'You have to have more patience, naughty boy.'

'It's a figure of speech. It means . . . Forget it. I have lots of patience.'

'Good.' She was back in seductress mode. 'I like men who are patient and slow.'

'I bet you do. Where are you?'

'I am in my car.'

'And where is your car?'

'In front of your building.'

'Oh.' I was genuinely surprised. Even for her, this was bold. 'Now who's being impatient?'

'I said I like it in my men,' she purred. 'I never said I was patient.'

'Well you'd better come in then.'

'I thought you would never ask.'

I stood at the top of the stairs waiting for her. She stopped three steps below me and leaned against the wall. She was wearing the same black jeans and white blouse she had worn to the office, with a red jacket and scarf. She had short, spiky, blonde hair and intense green eyes. I put out my hand and she caught it, pushed herself lazily away from the wall, and walked past me into the flat, dragging me after her. Inside she settled into an armchair, crossed her legs, and folded her arms across her breasts, without taking her eyes off me or speaking a word.

'Drink?'

She nodded and raised an eyebrow at the whiskey bottle, lying on its side on the coffee table.

'It's my birthday.' *Explanation?*

She smiled, revealing perfect white teeth, framed by dark red lipstick. I had never noticed how straight they were.

'Hey. Michael. Why did you not tell me?'

'You didn't ask.'

She unfolded herself, stood, and walked slowly towards me, one foot placed directly in front of the other, hips swaying, like a model on a catwalk. Her head was tilted forward and she looked at me from underneath her eyebrows, long lashes sweeping, blinking slowly. She slipped her hands around my waist and pushed her hips against mine, smiling when she felt me hard against her.

'Hi, birthday boy,' she said, voice soft and low, her accent sounding suddenly sexy, 'I brought you a present.' She ran her tongue along my jaw and under my chin. 'Want to unwrap it?' She stepped away from me, letting her left hand fall to her side. With her right hand she undid another blouse button, and I could see white lace against the brown swell of her breast.

'Patience,' I said, 'I'll get us those drinks.' I walked past her, running a hand across her stomach and over her breast, and went to the kitchen. When I got back with a bottle of wine and two glasses she was nowhere to be seen.

'Petra?'

'Here.' Her voice came from the darkness of my bedroom. The light from the hallway caught her, sitting on my bed, her boots lying like two abandoned bludgeons beside her.

'You have got a present to unwrap, Mr Birthday Boy,' she said, lying back on the bed, her blouse falling open and her breasts, like twin thespians, choosing to make their appearance.

It would be wrong to say that I made love to her. I fucked her. On top, from behind, from beneath, standing, sitting, sprawling. Ferocious, like an animal. Driven. I didn't care for her and I didn't care. And when I was finished I went to the bathroom and stood for a long time, scowling at my reflection in the mirror.

I found her standing in the living-room, lights off, naked, a glass of wine in her hand, staring out the window at new rain dampening the fog. Red tail-lights moved across her face, making it difficult for me to read her expression. She didn't turn to look at me. I stood beside her at the window, following her gaze. She looped an arm around mine and put her head on my shoulder.

'So. How is the birthday boy?'

'I want you to leave.' The words came out flat, emotionless.

She pulled her hand away sharply, as if I had suddenly become hot. 'What?'

'Now. I want you to leave.'

'But I . . . ' Her words trailed away. I looked at her, proud German, confusion spreading through her like an ink stain.

'You what?' I sneered. 'I'm not looking for a girlfriend. I don't want companionship. It was sex, it was good, it's over. What else do you want from me?'

'*Du Scheißer*,' she whispered, aghast. 'I thought . . . '

'You thought what? That Maria had it good? That you'd like a piece of that? Tough. Now you know. Maria didn't have it so good after all.'

'Bastard,' she shouted, and slapped my face, hard. I could feel the heat from her blow mushroom across my cheek.

'Yeah. I reckon I am.'

She threw the wineglass across the room, where it shattered against the wall, and then swept from the room, short steps, arms and legs rigid with anger. I couldn't help but watch her bare buttocks wobble in the half-light from the window. I heard her struggle into her clothes in the bedroom, sobbing. I stayed where I was, as if planted, listening. Then she was gone, slamming the door behind her.

I didn't move for several minutes. I watched her from the window, climbing into her car, a bundle of excess clothing clutched to her. She threw the car into gear and sped away, past silent sentry streetlamps.

'Happy birthday,' I told my reflection in the glass. 'Bastard.'

Thirty-three today. I'm entering my Jesus year. Alone. *Mother and child are doing well.* Not any more.

# GIVE US THIS DAY

Claire stared at me. Disbelieving. 'Come again?'

I sat, naked, on the edge of the bed, staring back at her. 'You heard me the first time. Will you?'

She gathered the sheet around her, covering her breasts, and lifted her hand to push her hair out of her eyes. She looked confused, her forehead pinched. Perplexed. She looked away from me, across the bedroom. 'I don't know what to say.'

'Say yes.'

Her head snapped around. 'That's not what I mean. I know the answer, I just don't know how to say it.'

Her face was hard. Unexpected. The sheet had slipped down, revealing her left nipple. I realised what was happening, but, even still, felt an incredible urge to reach out and touch it. I resisted, dragging my reluctant gaze upward until I was looking directly into her eyes. 'But, I thought . . . '

'I know what you thought. Oh, Michael. I'm sorry. This was all just supposed to be a bit of fun. Can't we just leave it at that?'

'Christ, Claire. I just asked you to marry me.'

She stood up, taking the sheet with her, suddenly shy, and gathered her clothes from where they lay, abandoned on the floor. 'I'll be back in a minute,' she said, without looking at me, and headed towards the bathroom.

When I bent to retrieve my own clothes, I could smell our sex on my body. I could remember the urgency I felt in the car on our way from the airport. Clambering up the stairs, her bag over my shoulder, I reached in front of me and put my hand between her legs. She let out a startled yelp and ran ahead of me, giggling, waiting at the top of the stairs, hands outstretched against further molestation. I brushed past her and she stood behind me, reaching around and trying to get her hands inside my jeans as I stood unlocking the door. *Your ass is mine, Mister.* I had pushed her ahead of me into the bedroom, our lips locked together, dropping her bag at the foot of the bed, where it still lay unopened, undressing her as we went. She fell backwards, laughing, onto the bed and struggled out of her jeans, then reached up and pulled me down on top of her.

I sat now staring at my reflection in the mirror. My hair was flat on one side, pasted against my head, standing erect on the other, a monument to our lovemaking. Sweat glistened on my forehead. My face was still red from my exertions. I sucked in my belly, holding my breath, and shifted sideways to see my profile. Depressing. Too much German beer. I gave up, letting the air hiss through my teeth like a slow puncture. I could hear water splashing in the bathroom across the hall. I pictured her, bent over the sink, breasts swinging free above the porcelain, spine arched, sheet in folds around her feet as she rubbed soap on her sweaty face. The tap was shut off. I listened to the silence, gathering my thoughts. What had I been thinking? *Will you marry me?* Jesus.

I looked up to see her standing in the doorway, fully clothed. She leaned against the door frame, ran a hand through her hair, and sighed. I was suddenly conscious of my nakedness. I stood up and stepped into my boxer shorts, then pulled my tee-shirt over my head. Neither of us spoke. She smiled, stepped towards me, put her arms around my waist and lifted her face to mine. I kissed her softly on the lips. I could taste toothpaste on her breath. She had brushed her teeth, using my toothbrush. An intimate gesture. I cupped a buttock with one hand and fingered her ear with the other, my face a mask, or so I imagined. She buried her face in my shoulder and sighed again.

Finally, she spoke, breaking the silence between us. 'Do you really love me?' A soft, little girl voice, coming muffled from the depths of my sweaty armpit.

'Yes. I do.'

But I did not love her. I had realised it as soon as I spoke the words. *Will you marry me?* I had ached for her for the past two weeks. I had missed her, telling myself that everything would be all right as soon as she was back with me. I counted the days until today, the hours until I found myself at the airport, the minutes until her plane touched down, the seconds until I saw her, lugging her bag through the arrivals gate, spotting me in the crowd, recognition, face lighting up. She had thrown her arms around my neck and wrapped her legs around my waist, kissing my face and squeezing me until I thought that I would pass out. I couldn't wait to get her back to my bedroom. I peeled her underwear off and entered her, rough, violent, violation. I wanted her, I needed her, I lusted after her. But I did not love her.

Her face reappeared, wrinkled forehead a question mark. 'Why did you ask me to marry you, though? I didn't take you for the marrying kind.'

I kissed her lightly on the cheek, released her, untangling myself, and sat on the bed. 'I don't know, you know? I suppose I thought that it would be the only way to get you to stay with me.'

'I'm not going anywhere.' She stood, one leg across the other, hands behind her back, head cocked to one side, with a little grin on her face.

'No, I mean here. Germany.'

Her brow wrinkled again, mouth pursing into a perfect circle, searching for the right words. 'Michael, this is a fling. It's a very nice fling, don't get me wrong, but it has a definite best before date.' She sat down beside me and took my hand in hers. 'There was a time, you know. I would have followed you anywhere. When you left, I couldn't believe you didn't ask me to come with you.'

'I wasn't ready for that kind of commitment.'

'Bollox, Michael,' she smiled at me and squeezed my hand, 'I know you too well. You can't fool me. I met your mother in the main street two months after you left and she told me you were living with this Maria one. How do you think that made me feel? I heard it from your mother, for Christ's sake.'

'Sorry. I should have called you.'

'Yeah, you should have. But you didn't. Anyway, the point is, you're the kind of guy who moves from one relationship to another. What do they call it? Serial monogamist? Whenever the net starts to get too tight you move on.' She paused, the smile slipping off her face. She studied our hands, working her fingers between mine. I watched her bite nervously at her lower lip. She pulled my hand into her lap, my body swivelling towards her. I found myself looking straight into her face and looked down at my feet, unable to meet her eye. 'You don't really want to marry me, Michael. Do you?'

'I suppose not.' My bare toes wriggled on the carpet, holding a certain fascination for me.

'The truth is, you're lonely. You want me to stay here and mother you, mind you, look after you. You want someone to sleep with you, cook for you, clean for you, and listen to you. But that person is interchangeable, Michael. I don't mind doing it for a while. I'm even enjoying it. But I know you, Michael Dwyer. If you think I'm going to agree to marry you and let you lead me up the garden path until, one morning, you wake up and decide it's time for a change, forget it. If, however, you want good sex and a bit of a laugh for a while, then I'm all yours.'

She swung her leg across me, straddling me, and pushed me back down on the bed. Gathering my tee-shirt in her fist, she leaned in very close to my face, squinted at me and hissed, 'You hurt me more than anyone ever hurt me, you bastard. Don't think for a minute I'm ever going to let that happen again.' Then she kissed me full on the lips, forcing her tongue between my teeth, and pinched my left nipple until a tear ran down the side of my face and blossomed on the sheet.

I can hear her breathing. Soft gasps punctuating darkness. I picture her, mouth open, slits of white showing beneath semi-closed eyelids. She is like a radiator under the sheet. Waves of warmth crash across me. I sense an arm close to mine. Fingers stretching, I touch her flesh. Warm, bare leg. She groans, mutters and turns away from me. I move closer to her, put an arm around her from behind, soft breast filling my hand. Then she is half awake, protesting. *Not now.* I feel her push my hand away. My arms encircle her again, hungry mouth caressing the back of her neck. Her voice comes, angry. *I said not now.* She pushes me away, harder. She does not want to be convinced.

Moonlight penetrates the bedroom, bathing it in blue. Pale green numbers tell the time. Four-thirty. I am fully awake now, far from sleeping. I sigh, sit up and swing my feet to the floor. One last look over my shoulder at the sleeping bundle, softly snoring now. I rise and leave the room, gently pulling the door closed behind me.

The tiles on the bathroom floor are cool, a day's heat dissipated in darkness. I wince as the light snaps on. It takes my eyes a minute or two to grow accustomed to the light. White face in the mirror. Mine. Sunken eyes. *Do you know what you're looking for, Michael?* How could I?

I think of Claire, asleep in the room across the hall. Innocent, childlike. Maria once slept there. Trusted me. *Interchangeable.* Claire's word.

'Do you even like yourself?' I realise that I am speaking aloud. My reflection looks back at me, unblinking. There are no answers.

Cold water, fresh on my face, shocks away the last of sleep. I rub a hand across my jaw. Black bristles. The weekend ends tomorrow. I'll drive her to the airport, we'll kiss in the departures lounge. 'Call me later, okay?' Her hand will brush my cheek. She will walk away, hand luggage only, carry on, enough for one weekend. She will turn to wave goodbye when she hands her passport for inspection. One last wave. Perhaps she'll blow a kiss. Then gone. And I will be alone. I can't live like this.

'Christ, Dwyer.' My face smiles crookedly at me from the mirror. 'Marry me? You stupid fucker.'

I snap the light off. Blink. When my eyes open my reflection has been replaced by darkness.

I ease myself back into the bed. *Careful. Quiet. Let her sleep.* She stirs, muttering. A cold arm, uncovered, finds its way across my chest. Warm breath in my face. A sleepy voice, semi-conscious, 'Goodnight. I love you.' *You won't remember that tomorrow, will you?* Hidden thoughts betrayed by sleep. I wrap an arm around her, sweet child, and cradle her head against my shoulder, soft brown hair tickling my chin. Her perfume permeates my senses, shampoo scent, soft skin. I hold a breath, wait for her to catch me, we breathe out together. Now we are in time. Close comfort. Soon I will sleep. But not yet.

January to March, known to perished peregrines, trudging through snow, as the suicide months, a time for survival. Frankfurt's sky stays grey, unbroken. Endless winter. Blood freezes in your veins. Unearthly cold. Unnoticed. Life goes on. Ireland cannot prepare you for this. There, snow means days away from school, a dearth of electricity. Snowmen . . . At most a tiny hiccup here. Paths are cleared by seven every morning. Cars slew workward with salt-streaked flanks. Old ladies stand, shovels in hand, at the ready. Waiting for the next snowfall.

It was beautiful in December. Fairy lights and *Glühwein*, the promise of Christmas. And memories. Maria pleading to be taken to the *Weihnachtsmarkt*. The ghost of Christmas past.

This will be my last year here. Maybe. I said the same a year ago. Then spring struck, without warning. Waking to birds singing, we sat on the balcony, drinking coffee. She turned to me, huddled in a woolly jumper, smiling through the weak morning sunshine. 'It's not so bad here after all.' She's gone now. I persist.

It is dark in the apartment at six o' clock. The only light is snow glow from outside. Someone revs an engine. Snowbound. The terrified scream of an urban animal weakening in quicksand. Headlights sweep across the window, creating a kaleidoscope of snowdrop shadows that slither down the wall. I lie on the floor, spreadeagled, warmed by water pipes snaking underneath the tiles. Stillness. Solitude secured.

It is hard to think of her now. Her softness. Swollen stomach, heavy breasts. The baby will be born soon. Small hands, fingers spread against stretched skin. *Feel it kick, Michael. Life. A part of you, father.* A part. Apart. Father. I would have been, but I have sacrificed the right. My stubbornness, a sleeping dog, was roused with grievous consequence. An opportunity missed. A chance of happiness. But here's a thought: maybe for the best. What kind of father would I make? Impossible to say. And maybe I will never know, there are no second chances. Too late. You can't go back.

Claire will come again this weekend. We will shiver through the streets together, wrapped against the foreign climate, foreigners. I will wonder what she's thinking, stranger, and keep my thoughts to myself. In school we wrote each other notes. Children's crayon scrawl. Spurious scraps of sentience, written surreptitiously. I thought I knew her then. I was a child. Aware of her, no more, no less. As a child, that was enough. We grew together, learning. Intense, intimate pubescence. I discovered myself through her.

Natural, then, that I should run to her. Quivering, screaming, questioning. Falling foul of falsehoods, confused by self-styled myths, I was in need. Claire was seventeen for me, or seven or eleven. I clung to her, cowering, afraid to face the world. She seemed to lead me back to solid ground. Another fantasy. *Michael falls the second time.* For Claire had grown without me. Woman from a child. I should have known. *Too late. You can't go back.*

*Time. So much time. Nothing to worry about. Time is on my side. Time to learn the lines, perfect my craft. I am a skilled performer. Nothing to worry about. Learn the lines. You learn them. Learned them. Didn't you?*

*Slip. I step onto the stage, actor. Arc-lights lock, white light, alive. Like sunshine splinters, bright, it leaves me blinking. I am tiny here, transfixed. Audience already? Thunder fades to silence; scattering like pearls, fresh fallen from a string. Nervous expectation. Wait. For me.*

*'Whose line? Mine?' But I'm not ready. Prompt, terse whisper, tells me what to say. 'But I'm not ready.' Panic grows, painful. Silent inside. Shuffles now. A cough or two. Time skips a beat. Come out again. Or hide behind the curtain. They will know. 'Whose line? Mine?' But I'm not ready.*

'Michael?' Claire's hand touched my face, a lifeline, dragging me from deep sleep. I opened my eyes and looked at her, confused, vivid afterimages burning, alternative reality.

'Oh Christ.' I sat up in bed, unsure, reluctant.

'That's a nice good morning.' She smiled at me across the breakfast tray. 'Wake up, will you?' She put the tray on the floor beside the bed and went to open the window. 'It stinks in here.'

'Jesus.' I struggled from beneath the blankets, rubbing at my eyes and scowling. 'Did you ever have one of those dreams? You know the ones that, when you wake up, you're not sure what's real.'

She lifted her tee-shirt, flashing her breasts at me. 'Real.'

I laughed, stretching a hand towards her. Too slow. She skipped beyond my reach. 'Come here. I'm awake now.'

She smiled at me, amusement dancing in her eyes. 'You'd be lucky. So tell me all about this dream.' She came and sat beside me on the edge of the bed.

'I've been having the same one over and over recently. I'm in a play or something, leading role, and I find myself on stage in front of this huge audience and I haven't got a clue what my lines are or even what the play is about.'

She bent to retrieve the tray, balancing it on the bed between us. 'I didn't know you were into dreams.'

'I'm not.' The coffee smelled good. 'I never used to dream at all. Now, suddenly, it seems that I dream every night. This particular dream more often than not. I'm waking up with panic attacks. Christ. Either I'm getting old or I'm drinking too much.'

'Maybe it's a bit of both.' She leaned across the toast and orange juice and kissed my cheek. 'Try not to think so much, you'll hurt yourself.' She patted my chest. 'Now listen, you. I'm flying out of here in a few hours' time so you'd better start paying me some attention.'

'Sorry. Thanks for breakfast.'

'*Bitte*. See? I'm learning. Hang on. I'll be back in a

minute.' I could hear her humming to herself as she made her way to the kitchen. Happy. I thought about my dream. How real it seemed, floundering on the stage, a step away from hysteria. Afraid of being found out. I took a sip of coffee. Scalding.

'Can you bring some more milk, Maria.' Shouting.

She appeared in the doorway, a bottle of *sekt* in her hand, face fallen. 'Claire.'

'What?' I realised, too late.

She leaned against the wardrobe. 'My name is Claire. You called me Maria.' Her voice was flat, emotionless.

'Oh Jesus. Claire. I'm sorry. I didn't mean . . . I'm sorry.'

'It's okay. Can you open this?' *Move on. Nothing to be gained here.* She held the bottle out to me, her voice still dull. *Damage done.*

'Claire. Come here.' She moved towards me and sat, listlessly, on the edge of the bed. I took the bottle and put it on the bedside table, then moved the tray around behind me. I put an arm around her waist, but she turned her face away when I tried to kiss her, leaving my lips against her hair. 'I'm sorry. Okay? Force of habit. It's hard to just remove someone from your life after so long.'

'You miss her, don't you?' She folded her hands in her lap and looked at the floor. 'Don't lie.' Just what I needed, another woman who could read my mind.

'Yes. Sometimes.'

She sighed. 'I thought so. It's all right, Michael. I don't mind. Not really. There'd be something wrong with you if you didn't.' She looked up at me and smiled sadly. 'Get over it, though. Will you?'

My turn to look away.

'There's more. Isn't there? Are you still seeing her?'

I looked at her sharply. 'No. I'm not. I swear.' But there *was* more. She had a right to know. I held my breath a moment, contemplating. She waited. I took a hand from the tangle in her lap, cradling it in both of mine. 'Maria is

114

going to have a baby, Claire . . . My baby.'

She began to cry, quietly at first, just tears slipping silently out of her, like mourners, heads bowed, following a funeral. And then her shoulders began to shake. She turned her face to me, dagger looks, hurt and hate attached to tear-strewn eyes. 'Why didn't you tell me? Michael. How could you not tell me?'

I clung to her hand, feeling her tug against me. If I let go, I felt that she would slip away, like a child's football at the beach, swept away on the tide, watched, helpless, from the shore. 'I meant to tell you. I would have . . . It never seemed . . . Appropriate.'

'Appropriate?' Snap. Her hand flew from mine. She stumbled away from the bed. Away from me. 'What would you know about appropriate, you selfish fuck?' She stood, bewildered, hands knotted in her hair. I couldn't help but notice her tee-shirt riding up, the dark triangle of pubic hair. 'Appropriate,' she spat. 'Oh Christ. That poor girl. How could you not tell me?'

I got out of bed and stood naked before her. 'Claire, I'm sorry.'

'Oh fuck off.' She raised a hand and thumped my chest. Once. Hard. 'Bastard. Now I know. You fucker. Can't commit to anyone. Not me, years ago. Not her, now. With a child on the way. You really are a prick.' She turned away and started to struggle into her clothes. 'How could I be such a fool?' She turned back to me. 'Here's one for the future, Michael. *My wife doesn't understand me.* Or are you already married? Did you forget to tell me *that* too?'

'No. I'm not. Not married.' I stood, hands at my sides, limp, watching her button her jeans.

'Can you call me a taxi, please.' . . . *You're a taxi, Claire . . . I forced the thought from my mind . . .* She stood, fuming, looking around at the clothes-strewn floor. 'I can pack while I'm waiting.'

'I don't want you to go, Claire.'

'Tough.'

I felt hard done by, wronged. 'For Christ's sake, Claire. I didn't know. All right?' I bent and picked my boxer shorts from the floor, where they lay abandoned from the night before. 'When I contacted you again I didn't know she was pregnant. That's not the reason we split up.'

'You wouldn't know the truth if it stood up and bit you on the arse, Dwyer.'

'Fine. Believe what you want. She only told me after we split up. What do you think I should do? Try to pretend everything is okay because she announces she's up the pole?'

'Charming. Up the pole? Whose pole, Michael?'

We stood staring at each other, her with her hands on her hips, head thrust forward, me holding my boxer shorts in front of my genitalia.

'Okay,' I said. 'I'll drive you to the airport. It's hours before the flight, though. There's no point in going yet.'

'I want to go.' Belligerent.

'Suit yourself. You pack, I'm going to have a shower.'

I drove her to the airport, early. She would not let me wait. *Just drop me at departures.* I got out of the car and sat against the bonnet, watching her hitch her bag over her shoulder, my hair still damp from the shower. She zipped up her coat, studiously ignoring me, her breath freezing in the cold afternoon air. A recorded voice told me in three languages that I was in a set-down area only.

'I didn't lie to you,' I said softly.

'What?'

'I didn't lie.' She looked at me, face softer now, anger cooling in the pale March sunshine. 'I just didn't get around to telling you. It's not something I think about a lot. I try not to. If I did, it would drive me mad.'

She looked at her feet, biting gently at her lower lip. 'I'm sorry, Michael. Maybe I overreacted. It's just . . . ' She raised her eyes to mine. 'I can't believe you wouldn't tell me about something so important.'

'I should have. I'm sorry.'

'Yeah.'

She wore a black woollen hat. Her nose was red and runny. She sniffed and rubbed at it with a black-mittened hand.

'Come back to the apartment,' I said. 'Have something to eat with me.'

'No, Michael. I think it's better if I just go. You've got a lot of shit to work through. I'm just in the way. I'll see you around. Okay?'

'Okay. If that's the way you want it.' She turned to leave. 'Claire?'

She looked at me over her shoulder. 'Yes?'

'Don't go like this.'

She smiled and took a step towards me. She leaned over, gathering a fistful of my coat, and kissed me lightly on the lips. Then she stepped back, adjusted the weight of her bag on her shoulder, and winked at me. 'See you around, buddy. Don't think it hasn't been fun.'

I sat against the car, watching her walk away. Just before she got to the terminal building I shouted after her.

'Claire.'

She turned, leaned towards me, and put a hand behind her ear. A question mark in the distance.

'You've really got a great arse,' I shouted.

She smiled, removed a mitten, waved two fingers in my general direction, and mouthed 'asshole'. I laughed, pushed myself away from the car, and watched the building swallow her.

# THY FATHER AND THY MOTHER

Her mother called me on Friday, the twenty-fourth of March. 'Michael Dwyer?'

'Yes. Who is this?'

'It's a girl. She's calling her Sarah.' Mission accomplished, she replaced the receiver before I had a chance to respond.

Her fingers fascinate me. Tiny pink things with perfect nails. She grasps my thumb, holding on for dear life. I have never held a baby before. I sit still, stiff, afraid to move, ignoring a muscle jumping in my back, protesting against this unnatural position. Maria sits in her hospital bed, watching me carefully. She had seemed glad to see me, smiling a welcome. I could not believe it when she asked me if I wanted to hold this miniature miracle.

What feelings I have experienced in the past twenty-four hours. Prodigal son becomes prodigal father. Sarah was born at five past three on Friday afternoon. Maria's mother broke the months of silence one hour later, against her better judgement.

My head is bent towards my daughter, supplication. Her tiny eyes closed, button nose, she opens her mouth and screws her face up in an infant yawn. Black hair, pasted to her skull. *Little fat creature. You bring tears to my eyes.*

I glance at Maria, bent towards us, white nightdress, strange smile on her lips, eyes dreamy and far away. 'Thank God she didn't get my nose.'

Maria's smile broadens. She touches my arm. 'She has

your eyes. Wait until she opens them. They are so beautiful.'

'She's beautiful. Like her mother.'

She shrinks a little, fine lines appearing on her forehead, the smile diminishing, but still on her lips, her hand touching my elbow. An awkward silence pushes its way between us. The baby's even breathing is the only sound in the small room. I clear my throat, breaking the spell.

'This is unbelievable. I'm not dreaming, am I?'

'No. She's real, Michael. As real as you and me.'

'A part of you and me.'

'Yes.' She watches me carefully.

'I would have come, you know.' I shift slightly on the bed, twisting towards her. 'I would have liked to have been here.'

'I know.' She squeezes my arm. Familiar. We are almost family. 'I thought about calling you. I almost did. But . . . You know. Anyway, it was all a bit sudden in the end. And Mammy was great.' Surrogate mother. I was surplus to requirements. It stings.

Maria reaches down, pulling back the blanket to get a better view of Sarah, as if she is afraid that it *is* a dream. That if she closes her eyes her baby will disappear.

'Thank you.'

She looks at me, puzzled, her hand still touching Sarah's face. 'For what?'

'For calling me now. You didn't have to.'

'You had a right, Michael.'

'I suppose . . . But I would have understood. I'm grateful, Maria. I . . . Just that. I'm grateful. I know how hard it was for you.'

'Forget it, Michael.' She looks at Sarah again, her eyes falling away from mine. Her voice is flat. Emotionless. She knows where the monsters hide. A place to be avoided. 'Let's just put it behind us. I don't want to talk about it. Okay?'

'Okay. I'm sorry. I . . . ' Suddenly I am blinking back tears. The enormity of what we have accomplished strikes me. I find myself laughing and crying at the same time. 'My God, this is incredible, Maria. Jesus Christ, I'm a daddy.'

Irresistible emotion, she smiles again. She cannot help it. She knows how I feel. 'It takes a bit of getting used to.'

We are sitting there, our child between us, grinning at each other like a couple of imbeciles. I don't know if it is the emotion of the moment, the passion of parenthood, or the stunning clarity that explodes inside a mind from time to time, but suddenly I realise that I am deeply in love with this woman. I love this child. Together, they have made me whole. *Me*. Michael Dwyer. Man about town. Something has been stalking me, observing from the undergrowth. Oblivious, I went about my business. Empty. Ignorant. But I am a father now. Bound by blood. A family tie stronger than son. Married? No. But this is my wife's face inches from mine. Open. Smiling. This is my daughter in my arms. Sleeping. Safe. Secure.

It dawns on me, what I have been. Expatriate pilgrim. My life has been a series of disjointed vignettes. I have spent my time waiting for the next glittering piece of the mosaic to fall into place. For that is what it means to be a pilgrim. To progress in fits and starts. Long lapses punctuated by uncomfortable activity. To exist. To wait. Maybe tomorrow. Something solid. Maybe my life will begin. And all the time we slide away from stimulants. Afraid to feel. I have been careful until now. Languorous lethargy has set in, a living rigor mortis. I have grown detached, become immune. Expunged, I have been emotionally neutered. But now this eight-pound apocalypse impugns my impunity. How can I remain aloof, distant? What else is there for me now?

It is a moment. And as with every moment, it is followed by another. Which passes. Then here I am, a stranger in their midst. To take what is on offer, I must give everything that I am. And how can I do that? It is a weakness. Fear of the unknown? Perhaps. And perhaps a fear of knowing. Wife, daughter. Woman, child. Husband? Father? I am loath to take responsibility. Reluctant relative, I am afraid. Mutinous messages flit across my consciousness. Dormant phobias surface, rolling shadows lurking menacingly in cerebral vapour. The bundle in my arms grows heavy. *I am afraid.* Father, look at your daughter. See her grow. See her know. See her take your measure. Uncomfortable realisation dawns. I am not ready for this. Not now. *Sarah, I am sorry. Little one. Loved one. Daddy is lost. Daddy is searching. Daddy can't come home.*

Maria reads my mind. Her smile is gone now. There is pity in her gaze. 'It's not easy, Michael. I understand.'

'No. No. I'm fine. I'm just a little overcome, that's all.' A tear has slipped quietly from the corner of my eye. She brushes at it.

'That I can certainly understand.'

I am struggling. Fighting down waves of panic. Trying not to let it show.

'Listen. I have to go book into a hotel or something,' I say, handing Sarah carefully to her mother. 'I'll drop by later. Okay?'

There is disappointment in her face. She cannot hide it. I feel like dog-shit, but I cannot stay a moment longer. I can feel the tentacles again, snaking out, stretching, clutching at my heels. *That's it, Michael. Slink off into the sunset. Mighty heroic of you.*

This is how I meet my daughter. The next time I see her she is two months old.

*Dear Maria,*

*How do I explain? Being a father frightens me. But you know that, don't you? If it didn't there would be something wrong. So many things frighten me. It's hard to be macho with you. You've seen me face my demons. I cast around for words, Maria, but this is a world beyond my experience. In truth, I am lost. I don't know what to do.*

*I wish that I could speak to my father. Now, more than ever. If he could only tell me how it felt to hold me for the first time. Did his heart near stop? Like mine? Last time we held each other, him fresh from hospital, I felt awkward, ill at ease, arms around a stranger. Not his fault, no. He did his best. And that was never meagre. He tried to know me as a man, this child of his, his offspring. But I was a reluctant charge, I never made it easy. I saw it in his eyes, the pain, but I remained aloof. I was skilled at parent patronising.*

*If I did this to him, this solid man, what chance have I? Oh God, I am afraid to be a parent. Old, she may spurn me, laugh at me, and mock my feeble bones. A full heart could not take that. It would burst. Therefore, I prefer to leave mine empty.*

*The picture lies before me on the table, extricated from its envelope. I turned your letter over and over in my hands before opening it. I lifted it to my nose, and sniffed, thinking to catch a scent of you. Nothing. At last I tore it open, and the photograph fell free. I stood, looking down at your face, beside my daughter's, on the floor. You were right, her eyes are mine. The rest of her is you.*

*I read the lines you wrote, Maria. A few of them were true. But I do write, I think of you, and I'm sorry that I hurt you. How were you to know? These words of explanation stay in bundles by my bed. Consolation, not for you, for me.*

*Sarah? Yes. I like the name. And she should grow like you. But I cannot be father to this imp. My seed, Maria. Nothing* more. I give the child to you. And when she asks about me, if she does, tell her what you want. Tell the truth, Maria. Tell her that I was consumed by fear, a fear that overcame me. Tell her I was weak and you were strong.

I wish that it was different, that I could be the man you need. But I cannot be other than I am. I've tried, Maria, straining, I have done my best to change. But my wickedness prevails, despite my efforts. I am a lost cause. Deep in my despair, however, you are still the light. And Sarah. Something good that I have done.

I will not sleep tonight. I will lie awake and miss you. From time to time, I will turn on the light. I will look at your picture, family, and wonder. What would it be like, to walk among the living?

*Michael*

Mine is a passive evil that manifests itself through inaction rather than action. I have come to know that. It does not make me proud. I harbour precious words, unspoken. Words to fill silences, like fingers in a wound to stop the bleeding. Compress. Compromise. But silence grows, infectious. Soon we will not speak at all. There is an edge to her now. Hidden things exposed, patience wearing thin. *I want to make it work, Michael.* But I have to want it too. Halfway won't work, she knows that now. And I can wait forever. As long as it takes. I can leave her hanging till it gets me off the hook. I don't need words to win this war of attrition.

I stand barefoot in the middle of my bedroom, rooted, telephone in hand, shoulders squared, ready for her onslaught.

She tries again, 'She's your daughter too. I'm just trying to do what's best for her. We should both be there, don't you think? And what about your mother?'

*Don't try to browbeat me, Maria. No surrender. Wait.*

'Michael? Are you still there?'

Pause. Thinking. 'Yes.' Nothing more.

'Jesus, you are so infuriating.' Tension in her voice.

'Sorry.'

I can almost hear her counting. Deep breaths. One . . . Two . . . Three . . . 'Well, when can you make it?'

'I don't know. Sorry.' Helpful as ever.

She sighs at me long distance, exasperated exhalation whistling in my ear. 'I don't know why I bother . . . Michael, your name is on the birth certificate. You should be at the christening. Don't you agree?'

'Of course. Yeah. Sure.' No argument. Nothing for her to seize on.

'So?'

'What?'

'Oh, for God's sake. When can you make it?'

'I told you, Maria. I don't know. Sorry.'

The bed looks inviting. I seem to spend so much of my

time travelling these days. I used to be able to sleep anywhere, and with anybody, but lately I have developed an acute case of antisocial insomnia.

Another effort. 'I'm trying to play fair, Michael, but you're not making it easy.'

'I'm doing my best. Okay?'

'No, Michael, you're not. Do you have to be so obtuse all the time? It's your daughter we're talking about here. You could make an effort.'

I could. I know that she is right. Why am I doing this to her? Haven't I done enough? Yet, after all the heartache I have caused her, she is still prepared to let me be part of her daughter's life. *Our daughter's life.* For some reason, not even known to me, I want to make it difficult for her. Confused, I hold the trump card. Suddenly uncomfortable, I find it hard to put an end to us. *Maria. I want you in my life. Even after all of this, I still want you, somehow, in my life.*

'I will, I will. Look, I don't mean to be awkward. I'll try to find a date that suits. Okay? Give me a couple of days. I'll call you back.'

I work an opening. A way back. Pushed to the brink again, bordering on breaking, she hesitates, wondering. 'Okay, Michael. Call me back.' She is resigned. For Sarah. Best for Sarah. 'Goodnight, Michael.'

'Goodnight. Kiss Sarah for me.'

'Don't I always?'

*Do you? Sweet. More love than I deserve.*

'Bye, Maria. I'll call you.'

'Goodbye, Michael.'

I am hanging up. I hear her voice, urgent, desperate. *Michael, Michael.*

'Michael. Are you still there?'

'Yes.'

She has, perhaps, sensed a softening in me. Fingernails. Clutching at straws. 'Michael . . . It's just . . . Sorry. Nothing really. Just goodnight.'

'Okay. Goodnight.'

'I love you.' Her voice seems to trail away. Little girl lost. Afraid of what I might say.

'Yeah. Me too.'

When she is gone I sit on the edge of the bed in the gathering gloom. *Goodnight. I love you.* I can feel a frown make furrows in my forehead. *Yeah. Me too.* Reflex? Recognition? I meant it when I said it. I mean it now. *Me too.* I love you, Maria. God help us. I sit alone on my bed. Foreigner. *Auslander.* I think of you, putting our baby in her cot, rocking her to sleep. Soft, lovely lullaby. Single mother. Singing. Home. My home? I honestly don't know. *Give me a couple of days.* Time to think. *I love you.*

Some things never change. Wexford is one of them. Solidly familiar. Stoic.

I lie. Wexford has changed. I do not recognise it any more. It is full of unfamiliar buildings and people I don't know. It is not the town that I grew up in. At night I can sit in a pub, nursing a pint of Guinness or warming a straight Jameson with the palm of my hand, and there is a dark familiarity. The flat, nasal accents dredge up distant memories and stir sleeping spectres. I lurk alone in the shadows, anonymous, in splendid isolation. And then a face from the past appears around a corner from another narrow street. *Howaya, Mick?* I am never given time to answer. I am a well known stranger here. Wexford owns me, but I do not belong. Michael Dwyer is yesterday's news. When you go, you go. If you turn your back on Wexford, it turns its back on you.

So why did I leave? I have asked myself that question over and over again. I have an answer. Polished. *I valued my privacy, a luxury in short supply in every small town in Ireland.* No. Fuck. Why should I lie? Priests preached to ignorant innocents. Fertile minds retained half-truths. How many prodigal children were created? *Fatten the calf, Dad. I'll be home when I'm home.* Why did I leave? Why does anybody leave? If you don't leave, you can't come back. *Michael Dwyer returned to Smallesville, resplendent in designer clothes and flushed with his success. His Porsche throbbed beneath his arse, his wallet weighed heavy, close to his heart. His heart skipped a beat as he gunned the engine and drove along the quays, meeting with . . . Nothing . . .*

. . . Nothing. Wexford forgot me while I was away. Or at least forgot how to care about me. Once upon a time, everybody knew everything there was to know about me. They still know. Maybe. They just don't care. And then I didn't want to go there any more. Little town, little people. I left you all behind. Until now.

I sat on a bollard on the wooden works, sunlight bouncing off my shoulders, watching children carefully placing pennies on the train tracks. We used to do that, burning our fingers on the flattened metal in the wake of the Rosslare-bound train. I remembered an afternoon, lying on the sun-warmed boards with my head on Teresa Foley's stomach, safe in the knowledge that the Intermediate Certificate exams were gone, never to return. I remembered mad Matty Brown, ten years old, covered in mud from head to toe, fiercely cycling along the quay towards his backyard in William's Street with the old tyre he had just retrieved from the mudbanks strapped to his handlebars. I remembered pushing him off the quay in the first place. I remembered making up with him so that I could come over and use his new swing.

I rocked the pram absent-mindedly with my foot, Sarah long since having drifted off to sleep. Maria crossed the road with two ninety-nines from Duffy's shop. When she handed me mine, the ice-cream was already beginning to run down the cone. I quickly licked around the edges and then submerged the chocolate in the melting mess.

'Thanks.'

She had a blob of ice-cream on the end of her nose. I reached over and wiped it away with my thumb, my fingers resting on her cheek. She smiled at me, to soften the blow, then gently pulled away. I let my hand hang there for a moment, then retrieved it, stuck my thumb in my mouth, and sucked off the vanilla-flavoured residue. She bent down to Sarah, adjusting the hood of the pram to keep the sun off her pink skin.

'I really appreciate this, you know,' I said.

'Your mother had to meet Sarah sometime.' She straightened up, glanced at me, then returned her attention to her ice-cream.

This trip was proving to be awkward. We were barely on speaking terms. She had called me during the week, suggesting a trip to Wexford so that my mother could see her two-month-old granddaughter. It was probably an effort

128

to fend off an inevitable visitation by my mother. I flew home almost immediately and rented a car at the airport. The trip down had been difficult. Long silences punctuated by polite small-talk, sometimes starting promisingly, then fizzling out. Uncharacteristically warm May sunlight streamed through the windows of the rented Nissan Micra, prompting agreement on an ice-cream break as we swept across Wexford Bridge.

Her blond hair fluttered slightly in the gentle breeze. I watched her pink tongue dart in and out, neck thrust forward, face a study of careful concentration. She wore a faded denim jacket, about four sizes too big, with the sleeves turned back over a mustard blouse. A stray rivulet escaped the cone and flowed down her hand. She moved the cone from one hand to the other, licking away the spillage and sucking her sticky fingers. She stood there, absent-mindedly holding a fingernail between her teeth, staring across the harbour towards the thin white strip of sand that marked the Raven's Point.

'You didn't have to come, you know?' I said.

'I know.' She didn't look at me. Her voice was distant, thoughtful.

'I have to say, buying me ice-cream and everything goes above and beyond the call of duty. Does this mean I'm back in the good books?' I stretched out a hand and caressed her elbow.

She seemed to come to life suddenly, shivering, like someone had just walked across her grave. She walked over and dumped the remainder of her ice-cream into a rubbish bin. Wiping her hands briskly with a paper handkerchief, she stared at me long and hard.

'Always looking for an angle, Michael, aren't you? Let's just say you shouldn't get too used to having us around, okay? Now let's get this over with.' Her voice was hard, bitter. She released the safety catch on Sarah's buggy and bounced off along the bumpy boards. Taking Sarah in her arms, she stood waiting for me beside the car. I sighed. Not in the good books after all.

Perhaps sensing her mother's foul mood, or maybe just cranky at having been woken so unceremoniously, Sarah began to cry. I unlocked the door for them and folded the buggy into the boot. Maria sat in the passenger seat, Sarah on her knee, comforting the sobbing child. I slammed the door as I got in, beginning a fresh round of shrieking. Maria flashed a wicked glance in my direction. 'Oh, for Christ's sake.'

I was annoyed. I felt like joining in with Sarah's wailing. 'Look, this was your idea,' I said, spitting the words between clenched teeth. 'Can we at least try to be civil to one another until we get back to Dublin?'

'Fine. I can be civil. Just don't talk to me unless you have to and keep your fucking hands off me.' Her eyes were on fire. She was shouting at me, frantically bouncing the weeping baby on her knee.

'Charming.'

'I had a good teacher.'

'Jesus.' I flung the car into gear and began to edge out into the traffic along the quay. Then, under my breath, I said, 'I should have stuck with Teresa fucking Foley.'

Sarah roared on. Maria just glared at me from the passenger seat.


We sit in my mother's kitchen. Her haven. When does she venture outside this room? Bed? Does she sleep now? It does not look as though she does. Dark half-moons of flaccid flesh hang heavily below dull eyes. Shopping? Tins pack presses, storm shelter, well stocked. Someone must deliver. Left alone, she stays alone. Deserted wife. When do you go out? Once a week? Sunday morning sacrament. Christ have mercy.

Her pale face lights up when she sees us. *I have been expecting you.* Understatement. *I have lived for this moment since your phone call.* Arthritic arms outstretched, she brushes past me, eyes only for her granddaughter. *Sarah, meet my mother. Grandma. You would have loved your granddad, but he's gone now. Oh my, how he would have loved you.* Maria hands her over. Old arms encircle delicate descendant. *Look at you, little one.* Look at *you*, Mother. Rejuvenation. Feeding from this infant. She has given you life again. Maybe she will give us all life again. *Come in. I've just put the kettle on.*

She sits in her kitchen with the baby in her arms, cooing and clucking like a mad thing. Maria and I sit at opposite ends of the table, solid pine between us.

'You look tired, Mother.'

She raises her face for a moment, eyes sparkling behind thick lenses, Sarah pulling at the chain dangling from her spectacles. 'It must be the excitement, I didn't sleep much last night.'

Glasses. New. Another nail in her coffin. Must everything let you down? Your bones? Your eyes? *Your son?*

I glance at Maria and catch her looking at me. Does she see my pain? I mould my features. Mask. *The pain belongs to me, Maria. I own it. Mine alone.*

'Back in a minute.'

Minor exploration. Thick dust lies in the living-room. A month-old magazine lies open on the coffee table. The air is stale. Dust motes swirl in sunlight streaming through the window.

Maria finds me here, staring out the window. 'I thought I'd give them time alone. To get to know each other. You know?'

'Yeah. Good of you. Thanks.'

We stand, side by side. Her company does not feel awkward. It is comfortable, like an old sweater. When I look at her she smiles back at me. Apologetic. 'Sorry about earlier.' She is trying to find common ground again.

'No. It's me who should be sorry.'

She sighs and looks back out the window at the sunlit garden. 'We seem to spend a lot of time apologising to each other recently, don't we, Michael?'

I find myself smiling. 'Yes. I noticed.'

She takes my hand in hers, playing with my fingers, like she used to do when we were together. 'Sarah needs a father, Michael. I don't mean to be so pushy. It's just . . . Well. Sometimes you need to be pushed.'

Dearest Maria. Still trying to save me. Her fingers are cold against mine. My smile widens. 'Warm heart.'

'What?'

'Nothing.' She looks at me quizzically. 'Why do you still bother with me, Maria? After all I've done to you. Why?'

She studies my face. Genuine puzzlement.

'Don't you know?'

I do not reply.

'I love you, Michael. God knows why. I always will.'

We stand for a moment, holding hands, looking into each other's eyes as if seeking some great truth there, sunlight dancing between us. Then she breaks the spell. 'I'd better go check on Sarah. Your mother has probably had enough by now.'

'Maria . . . I . . . ' But I am too late. She is gone and I am speaking to the door, swinging shut behind her.

Inevitable? Maybe. Old feelings work their way to the surface, like a rash scratched at. *Leave it alone, child.* But you can't. When you know it's there, you can't. Pick at a sore until it becomes inflamed. Angry. Septic.

I saw it, God forgive me, and knew what I was looking at. I could pretend that I mistook the moment. Honourable intentions . . . No. I won't. For once I will tell it as it was. I saw a weakness in her and I took advantage. Egged on by the memory of sweat-soaked summer nights. Long, comfortable afternoons. Passion pulsing. I gave in to a selfish impulse. It was simple. I wanted her, and wanting was

132

enough. I took what I wanted, with callous disregard for what it might do to her. *I must plead guilty, m'lud. Temporary insanity cannot form the basis of my defence, for my insanity is of a more permanent nature. And my crime? Premeditated? Surely. As premeditated as a crime can be . . .*

*. . . So hang me!*

It was dark when we got back from Wexford. Sarah was asleep in the back of the car. Maria bent over her, unstrapping her from her car seat. A mother's hands, moving carefully over her baby. From my vantage point in the driver's seat, I watched her perfect profile, my desire almost tangible. A full day spent in close proximity. Watching her move. Seeing, from the corner of my eye, slow, sidelong glances at me as I drove, hand on the gear-stick, feeling the warmth from her body. Aching to touch her. *Careful, Michael. Take your time.*

'Let me help you.'

'That's okay.'

My eyes traced the curves of her body, hunger gnawing at the pit of my stomach. She lifted the sleeping child from the car and started towards the darkened house. *Mammy must be at the bingo.*

'Hang on. I'll help you.'

I got out of the car, unstrapped the baby-seat and carried it, with her bag, into the house. I knew. Of course I knew. I meant for it to happen. If I had not I would have left the car unlocked.

Maria snapped a light on in the hallway. Sarah stirred in her arms, her tiny face wrinkling with annoyance. She opened one blue eye, gave me a baleful look, sneezed, and settled back against her mother's shoulder.

'Thanks,' Maria whispered, 'drop that stuff anywhere.'

'That's okay, I'm not in any hurry. I'll carry them upstairs for you.'

She smiled her thanks and started up the stairs. I followed her to her bedroom and watched her settle Sarah in her cot. We stood for a moment, proud parents, hearts brimming over, and I covered her hand with mine. She looked at me, smiling, eyes full of tears.

'You must be tired,' I said gently. 'It's been a long day.' I leaned over and kissed her hair softly. She did not pull away, but her smile faded into a confused frown. 'Thank you. I'm sure it meant a lot to my mother.'

She smiled again, safe ground. 'Yes, it probably did.'

I looked into her eyes. 'It meant a lot to me.'

I leaned towards her. This time I kissed her lips. The softest, briefest caress. She stiffened slightly, indecision. I did not give her time to think about it. I coiled an arm around her waist and pulled her small body against my erection. She breathed a low moan. 'Michael, no.' But her words lacked conviction. Too late. She raised her face to mine, confusion seeping across her features. I kissed her lips again. Still softly, but this time lingering. I touched her lips with my tongue. Her mouth opened, moist, warm invitation. Letting go of her hand, I reached around and cupped her buttock in my palm. Her arms came up and over my shoulders and her body pushed against mine. She pulled my head down and kissed me with a passion that surprised me, biting at my lips, teeth tapping, tongue hard in my mouth. We somehow managed to undress each other from the waist down without coming up for air. My hands found their way under her tee-shirt, rubbing her breasts and bunching the muscles in her back. My erection tapped against her stomach. I lifted her off the floor and she put her legs around my waist. I carried her, like that, our lips still locked. When I threw her on the bed I saw her eyes. I can't deny it. They screamed at me. *Michael. Don't do this. If you're not going to follow through, don't do it. For God's sake, don't hurt me any more.* I pushed her backwards onto the sheets and forced myself inside her.

I knew. Damn me. I knew. Her eyes, her face, her body. They had all flashed the same message. *Give me a sign.*

*Want me. Give an inch and I'm yours.* I laid the trap. I baited. I waited. And when the chance came I took it. To what end? At the time it was an end unto itself. Both kneeling on the bed, her straddling me, we climaxed together, enantio-morphic. Spasmodic bodies jumping and crackling with electric energy and crumbling together in sated synchrony.

I wanted her. I took her. What reasons did I need? Her head on my shoulder, fingers drawing shapes on my chest. Not shapes. Letters. I-L-O-V . . . 'I'd better be gone before your mother gets home.' Excuses. *Put your pecker back in your pants, Michael, before it gets you in any more trouble.*

She raised her head. Dreamy. Little fist against her cheek, elbow on the sodden sheets, she watched me dress. Happy. Wordless. I buttoned my shirt and sat on the bed to tie my shoelaces. 'Gotta go.' I leaned over and kissed the top of her head. 'See ya, kiddo. We'll talk tomorrow.'

She called me. I turned in the doorway, looking at her lying naked on the bed.

'Yeah?'

'I missed you. You know I love you, don't you?'

I smiled at her and winked. 'Yeah. Me too. See ya.'

'Bye. Call me.'

I turned and made my way down the stairs. It was raining outside. I hunched my shoulders and ran across the street to the car. I climbed into the driver's seat and blew a long, deep breath at the windscreen. *We'll talk tomorrow.* I looked at my eyes in the mirror. 'Asshole.' Unlike Michael Dwyer, tomorrow never comes.

Maria leans towards me, eyes closed tight in concentration. Her hand rests on my chest, maintaining contact but holding me at arm's length. A battle rages. When words come, her voice is calm, steady. 'That isn't what I meant, Michael. Please don't make this any more difficult than it already is.'

Her eyes open slowly, blue orbs searching. *What do you*

135

*need to see in my face?* Not found. Tears trickle. Long liquid lines mark her face. Emotional bruises. Testament. Battered woman, without being beaten. *Do you feel shame, Michael? Do you?*

I look around the hotel room, anywhere but at her. The bed is a mess. We were about to make it, Maria always embarrassed to leave sheets strewn every which way. Her hair is still wet from the shower, her towel is draped across the back of a chair. Late afternoon sunlight streams through the open window, accompanied by city sounds four floors below.

She is speaking again. Distant words. I hear them, like an eavesdropper, as if they are not intended for me. 'I don't want to exclude you from my life. Or Sarah's. But this time it's you who have to do the running. I'm not going back to Germany. If you want to be with us, you have to be with us here.'

She is waiting for an answer. Say something. I hear my voice. 'You know that I would if I could. But it's not that easy. I don't belong here.'

Ah, but she knows me so well. Sidestepping, Michael. Look at her eyes. See the glimmer? She knows. Still searching for emergency exits. You should have been a fire prevention officer. Words form in her stomach and work their way up her oesophagus, spilling into her mouth. She clenches her jaw against them, lips vanishing into a thin line of self-control. I imagine them, wild words, hurtling about inside this cavern, bouncing off her tongue and hammering on her teeth. And just when she has gained control, they curl together in one foetal ball which begins to grow. The size of an egg, it forces her teeth apart. Muscles strain. She will not give in. Force it down. Fight it. Kill it. But it pops her open like a pea-pod, toxic bile spewing forth, projectile-vomited vitriol.

'Jesus fucking Christ. Bastard. Shithead. Oh my fucking

God. Christ. Fuck. How could I be so God-damned fucking stupid? Stupid. Stupid. Bitch.'

She is spinning away from me, fist to her forehead, eyes bulging, spitting streams of caustic self-abuse through clenched teeth. I catch her arm, jerking her back to face me.

'Stop for fuck's sake.' Screamed at point-blank range.

She stops, as if slapped, sucking in a breath. Fear dissolves her anger. Fear of me? Fear of herself? Her body is small and fragile, endangered by my grip. I relax my fingers, afraid of hurting her. *Afraid of hurting her? What do you think you've been doing all this time?*

Her voice is small now, squeezing through her pain. 'Jesus. How could I let you get close to me again? How?'

Her eyes are wide. There is a look of wonder on her face. It is as if now, this very minute, she has realised for the first time that Michael Dwyer is a total, unadulterated, make-no-mistake-about-it, irredeemable bastard. She shakes her arm loose, pulling away from me.

'It's not that easy,' she says, gathering herself together. 'I won't let it be that easy for you.' She is salvaging her injured pride, beginning to realise that it is me who is to blame. 'You don't want to give an inch, Michael. Do you? You think you can just waltz in here and play with me any time you want. Wham, bam, thank you ma'am? Not likely. Not again.'

'I just . . .'

'What?' Why should she let me try to explain? She has heard it all before. 'You don't belong here? That's a heap of crap, Michael. Don't belong where? With me? With your daughter?'

'That's not what I'm saying.' Oh, but it is. She knows.

'What are you saying then? Tell me. Where? Where do you belong?'

In Malé, two brown children chase a yellow balloon, white teeth flashing in the bright sunlight, oblivious to their squalid surroundings. Hearts aching, we look at each other, then turn our sunburnt noses towards the harbour, where we sit waiting for our dhoni to take us from this township and deliver us unto five-star luxury, half an hour away. *Shall I stah yah coffee, Sah?* Where do I belong?

In Varese, sun-bronzed and beautiful we browse through the stalls in the marketplace. Lord and lady. She sees a shirt she likes. Bright blue stripes on white cheesecloth. *How much? I don't speak your language.* I drive a hard bargain. As we turn to go, two hundred-lira notes are pushed into my hand. *'For coffee.'* Weather-beaten Italian faces laugh and smile as we walk away, clutching our prize. One hour later, I see the same shirt in a shop next to the hotel for half the price. Where do I belong?

In Malta, the bus driver stands on the brake. Abandoning his post, he scuttles back along the road and retrieves an empty bottle from a rubbish bin. It is worth a few precious Maltese pennies. Climbing back aboard, he gives me a gap-toothed grin, raising his trophy so that I can see it properly. *Look. Look.* He retrieves his seat and throws the bus into gear. We trundle on to Valetta. Where do I belong?

Rome. I take a bus from Termini, squashed in a squabble of locals and tourists. The Vatican is mobbed by a salt-and-pepper crowd of priests, nuns and nobodies. I stand looking at the upturned faces, gazing in adoration at the miracle of Michelangelo. How could I not be impressed? Did I find my faith? Perhaps. Momentarily. Where do I belong?

I stand on Ayer's Rock, alone among the tourists. Red desert stretches to the Olgas. Proud. I did it. Reached the giddy heights. Down to earth. Knees ache. Sunlight beats against my back. *Christ. I'm almost there.* I stand at the bottom, looking up the way I've come. Chain swinging, heaving line, like ants. 'Sacred ground,' an aboriginal tells me in the bar. 'How would you like it if I hammered in crampons and climbed your Notre Dame cathedral?' Where do I belong?

A child cries. A storm comes. A truth reveals itself. A spell breaks. And Michael would just as soon not be there. If you don't belong, you don't have to stay around to take the consequences. The pilgrimage continues. Where do I belong?

Maria stands, looking at me, as if I can answer her question. I stare back, blankly.

'Are you going to answer me?'

I say nothing. It feels as if, by being perfectly still, I can avoid this predator. There is silence. She waits. She exhales. A long, low sigh. She plucks her bag from the table. 'I suppose not.' Her voice is weary, spent. She turns in the doorway, looking back at me. She smiles, but her eyes are frosty. 'By the way, Michael. Fuck you.' And then she is gone.

Do dreams count, Maria? If I could only sleep forever. The pilgrimage ends. I find happiness in the ether. Underneath the eiderdown. Safe. Warm. Woolly. Cotton-candy comfort. I am a child again. Trusting, honest, open. Life spoils, Maria. Expectation weighs heavily. *What do you want to be when you grow up?*

Germany suits me. It is a country without identity. Ashamed of what it was, afraid to be what it is. It is a magnet. Attracts the likes of me. Remember, returning once, you turned to me, fresh from slumber, drowsy, doe-eyed, as the plane swooped low over the autobahn? 'Nearly home,' I whispered, kissing your flushed cheek. You stretched, sleepy, and smiled at me. Red wrinkles, imprint of my jumper.

'No,' you said. 'Not home. We've just been home.'

I held your hand for landing. You used to be afraid. Remember? 'Well I'm home. Did you fasten your seatbelt?' Last word. Change the subject. That's me. Win the point and move on.

How many times did you talk about the future, Maria? Counting days until the end of another contract. I always won another. *Last one. This time I mean it.* Did you never guess? Or did you think that, given time, I would come to my senses? You hated this place. Anonymous. Cold. But I revelled in the anonymity. I thrived on it. Like Dublin years before. Nobody knew me. I could be anything, anybody that I wanted to be. *What do you want to be when you grow up?*

We fought for weeks before you met my parents. You wanted to know everything about me and could not understand my resistance. The mystery was important to me. I could re-invent myself with you. Speleologist, you prodded and poked at my private persona, seeking to gain entry to my soul. Nobody ever got as close as you, Maria. Did you know that?

Wexford welcomed you. I grew petulant, peeved by your acceptance. I felt less special. You began to love me. Baby pictures. *Wasn't he cute? What did he want to be when he grew up?* Is nothing sacred?

'Let's go home, Maria.'

'Home?' My mother lifts an eyebrow. A new edge to her. 'I thought this was your home.'

'No, Mother,' I know what I am about to do. 'I live with Maria. Our flat in Germany is my home.'

*Our* flat. Bombshell. Sin. *This woman stole your son.*

Maria's voice, horrified, 'I thought you knew. Michael? You said they knew.'

Too comfortable, Maria. I had to force an opening. You wanted to know me. This is me. Cruel. Vicious. Nasty little fucker. I had to take you away from them. To them, how could I ever be anything other than the little boy with short trousers and the short-back-and-sides, furiously pedalling his red plastic car. Always going somewhere, fast.

Years later we emerge from the airport car park. The autobahn is moments away. There are no speed limits here. My foot mashes the pedal to the floor and the car jerks forward. *Gerry and Eileen's first visit. Gerry sits up front with me. 'Jaysus, Eileen, he's doing two hundred and twenty.' Eileen breaks off mid-sentence, 'Relax, Gerry, it's*

*kilometres over here.' He is appeased. Briefly. Mental arithmetic.*
'. . . *Eileen?'* Always going somewhere, fast. Germany suits
me.

# THY WILL BE DONE

It seems I have a penchant for doorsteps. I ring another bell. Beggar. *Penny for the baby.* Bad penny. Always turning up.

Claire emerges, breakfast weary, sleep still clinging to her eyes. She is wrapped in her green dressing-gown, a white tee-shirt peering through the vee at her neck. Her face hardens when she sees me, mouth curling involuntarily, as if someone has placed something unsavoury before her. 'Michael.' She runs a hand through heavy hair. 'It's been a while. Again. Come in.' I need no second invitation to skulk across the threshold. In. She makes it all too easy.

'Toast?' She leads me to her kitchen, long legs, bare feet, toes curling through the carpet.

'No. Thanks. I've eaten.'

'Coffee then.'

'Sure.'

'Sit down.'

Sitting at her table, visitor, I am aware of her attempts to keep her back to me, loath to look, in case a random glance might give away too much. She busies herself with kettles and jars. Casual. Intensely.

'Claire?'

'Yeah?' She risks a look over her shoulder, guarded eyes. *You can do the work, boy.*

'I missed you. Okay? I don't know what else to say. Help me out here.'

She softens slightly. 'What about the baby? A girl. I heard.'

'Sarah. Yes. She's beautiful.'

'So what are you going to do about it?'

I sigh. 'She's a part of me, Claire, and I love her to pieces. But that's not the point, is it?'

'What *is* the point, Michael?' She speaks quietly, turning towards me. She leans against the sink. The kettle begins to boil in the background. Arms folded loosely in front of her, she holds a hand across her face. Shield. 'I don't mind telling you, I'm getting a bit pissed off. You seem to think that this . . . Jesus, I'm not sure how to describe it . . . Thing . . .? You seem to think that this thing between us can just be switched on and off whenever you feel like it. You are a very annoying person, Michael Dwyer. Do you know that?'

'Yeah. I'm beginning to get the picture. Listen. You were right. I had a lot of shit to work through. I know what I want now, Claire. I want you. Give me another chance. Please?'

My question hangs in the air between us, like a plum, ripe, ready to be plucked. She examines it, pausing, looking at it from another angle. Hesitant. The kettle, ignored, tired of spewing steam, clicks off and grumbles its way towards silence.

'What makes you think I'm still available?' She looks directly at me for the first time. Proud.

'Are you?'

A smile flickers on her lips. 'Maybe.'

I grin at her, village idiot. 'Claire. I'm sorry about the last time. I came back too soon. I should have sorted everything else out first. I'm ready now. Yours. Hundred and twenty per cent. Okay?'

'No such thing, asshole.'

'Okay, little Miss Pedant. One hundred per cent. My final offer.'

'Damn you, Michael. Why do I let you do this to me?' Her smile is bitter. 'I really should know better.' Tears fill her eyes and spill out onto her cheeks. A tissue emerges from her dressing-gown pocket and is used to dab at the moisture.

'Does this mean what I think it means?'

She sniffs and wipes at her nose with the tissue. 'You're on probation, you fucker. You'd better not hurt me again or I'll chop your balls off.'

'It's a deal.'

'Come here.' She spreads her arms, bare feet crossed, head tilted slightly to one side, long hair spilling on her shoulder. I am moving to her, smiling, when the similarity strikes me. Crucifixion.

Claire spends the summer teaching me. Making me let go, a little at a time. 'I am afraid to fall in love with you,' I tell her. Afraid. *Scaredy-cat*. She skips along a path in front of me, dappled in a German forest. Holds my hand at breakfast. *I'm giving up my job*. So weekends aren't enough. *I want to be with you*. Thunderstorms come rolling off the Odenwald at evening time, forcing us to shelter in the bedroom. Underneath the covers she protects me. Rain beats against the window. First drops, caught by her, mix with the sweat on her shoulders. White in lightning, she gasps and arches under me. How could I not love her?

\*

She fills my thoughts now, grabbing my attention. She has burrowed deep into my consciousness, compelling me to need her. I find myself holding her, breathing against her skin, her heartbeat loud in my ear, her hands running through my hair, and I realise that this would be enough. Tamed. I came to her in pieces. Patiently, she put me back together.

\*

Found sulking in the kitchen, I am encircled by her. Warm hands held against my chest, her chin resting on my shoulder. *Hey, buddy. What'cha thinking?* She will not let me drown here. Sucking beer from my bottle, she takes my hand and leads me to the living-room. Living.

\*

'This used to be a fling,' I say, kissing the top of her head. She nuzzles further into my shoulder, her soft breasts bare and warm against my stomach.

145

'Used to be. It's different now.' Her fingers rub softly at my nipple.

'What's different?'

'You are.' She climbs onto an elbow and kisses my lips.

*

Last plane. She cries in terminal two. 'I hate this.' Clinging to my hand.

'It's the last time, love,' I tell her. 'You'll soon be back for good.' They are calling her. Last remaining passenger. 'You'd better go.' Her tongue is soft in my mouth, her tears running down my cheek. We are becoming one.

'I can't bear to be away from you,' she says, holding me. 'I love you.'

'I know. Go on, now. I'll see you in a fortnight.' She peels from me, reluctant, puts a finger to my lips, and turns away.

*

A hasty trip to Ireland, picking up her things. Her parents watch in silence as she lugs her bags across the threshold. Come darkly to watch their daughter leaving home. I lean against the car. 'Is that all? Two bags?' I ask.

'No. I have another one inside.'

'Jesus. You travel light.'

She pats my cheek. 'That's the ticket, Mick. Travel light and take no prisoners.'

Loaded up, she hugs her mother. 'See you, Mam. Cheer up. It's not the end of the world. I'm only going to Germany.' Her mother sniffles, her father glares at me.

'I'll miss you,' her mother says. 'Sure you were only round the corner.'

'It's time I left home for real,' says Claire. 'Two streets away was cheating really.' She leans over and gives her father a peck on the cheek. 'Be good, Brenno.'

He looks like a bulldog shitting razor-blades. 'Are you sure you know what you're doing?'

'No.' She smiles at him. 'But if it's a mistake, at least it's my mistake.' He throws another filthy look in my direction. She glances at me. Troubled. She lowers her voice and puts a hand on his forearm. 'Please try to be happy for me, Daddy.'

Brendan Roche looks into his daughter's face. Her frown makes his heart ache. 'Of course, child.' Soft voice, choking with emotion. 'We're always here for you. You know that.'

I look at my watch, uncomfortable. 'Time to go, Claire.'

She looks at me, pleading. 'Just another minute, Michael.' She hugs them both again. 'Bye-bye. I'll call you.' Then she turns and walks resolutely to the car.

I hear her sniffing as I swing the car out of the driveway. 'No prisoners? Was that what you said?'

She looks at me through watery eyes, seeing my smug smirk. 'Go fuck yourself, Michael.'


Over dinner you turn to me, holding my hand under the table. There's something that you're bursting to tell me. I am awash with amusement. *What?* I ask you with my eyes. You squeeze my hand and turn back, bubbling, to our hosts. Later, in the car, you are giddy, intoxicated with excitement.

'What is it? You've been like a little girl all night.'

'Michael.' You are hugging yourself, elated.

'Yes?' I'm smiling, captivated by you. Waiting. Look at you. All smiles and shy innocence. 'What? What?' Impatient.

'I've decided.' Pause. I wait.

'Good. What have you decided?' Okay. A little prompting.

'That I love you.'

'I'm glad. I love you too.' We sit together, happy, following the headlights home.

'Michael.' Something more.

'Yes.' I glance at you, sitting sideways in your seat, studying me.

'Will you marry me?'

I laugh. Just once. 'Will I what?' You punch my arm, extended to the steering wheel.

'You heard me, Michael. Will you?' If we were standing you would stamp your foot. I smile at you.

'Of course I will.'

You squeal and clap your hands, then throw your arms around my neck.

'Claire. Look out. I'm driving.' And you retreat, glowing, to the passenger seat, your hand still on my shoulder. 'Jesus.' I shake my head.

'You're not going to change your mind?'

'No. Never.'

'I love you, Michael Dwyer.'

'What can I say? I'm a lovable kind of guy.'

We are betrothed.

*Poor child. Weep. I see you, what became of you. Nose flayed, flawed. A butterfly. Pinned. Spread. Open. Red gash across pink cheeks, tears diluting blood. Black eyes. Patchwork face. Mirrors promise pain now. Things to be avoided. Scarred. Disfigured. Marred. Poor child.*

*Do you hate me? . . . Sorry . . . Always me.*

*I was scarred too. My hand. They put the nail in. Knuckle crushed. I didn't know. Didn't feel it until later. Until the flames came.*

*Oh Christ. I am so, so sorry.*

Contrary to popular opinion, accidents rarely happen quickly. They stalk us. Moving furtively, they hide in dark spaces, lope along beside us as we move, oblivious, through tortuous paths. Inevitable, tragic, convergence. We see icebergs. Innocuous. Floating. Suspended between blues. Thinking to understand, we move slowly forward. Drawn. Confident. Fools. The larger menace lurks just beyond our perception.

Accidental? Counterpoint. The music of chance. What if? *I had let her drive. I had not turned towards her. I had not brushed at her hair. I had not paused to marvel at the miracle of her.* What if?

You are so beautiful. I pause, hand lightly touching your cheek, a smile on my lips to mirror yours. It is a moment. Frozen. Timeless. Whole. We are connected. Quietly, calmly, it dawns on me that I can let go of everything that has gone before. For an instant, you are enough. I feel a weight lift from my shoulders. A sigh escapes me. Tonight I am . . . happy.

And then your face changes, twists in horror. Your body tenses, eyes widen, mouth falls open to reveal a single, strangled warning . . .

. . . MICHAEL . . .

. . . jerking me back to here and now. I hear your scream as my head snaps around. My own voice roars in my head. *Fuck.* Eyes wild in the windscreen. Lips drawn back in terror. The wheel spins beneath my palms, feet stamping at pedals. *Christ. Jesus.* The car slews sideways. Too late. I do not hear the impact, I feel it in my chest. Blood rushes through my veins, trying to escape, pounding at my head. Tyres skid on gravel, a wheel escapes the road. Carnival. Spinning. Colour. Light. Then stillness, as the car settles on its roof.

A low moan escapes me, fracturing the silence. Other noises pierce my consciousness. A slow, steady drip behind us. Cooling metal pinging in the darkness. Claire sobs gently beside me. Alive. Thank Christ. The animal whimpers on the road. We hang in our harnesses, two bats. Blind. Mute. Helpless. My left hand feels strange, numb. I reach towards her with my right and touch her. She flinches and draws a wet breath deep into her throat.

'Claire?'

My voice sounds odd, unfamiliar. She does not answer.

'Are you okay, Claire?'

Still no answer, but this time her hand covers mine. It feels hot, sticky.

'I'm sorry, Claire. I'm so sorry.'

Words to live by. Words I live by.

I feel the slightest pressure in her grip for just a moment. Enough. We hang like that, holding hands, until the ambulance arrives.

First there are headlights. Cars. Somebody bends and shines a flashlight through the window. I squint at him. '*Zwei.*' He is calling back up the bank to his companions. '*Zwei Personnen.*' He asks in German if we are all right. All I can do is stare blankly at him. I hear him scramble back up the hill. The wait continues. Occasional muffled laughter can be heard. I picture them, huddled together in the beam of the headlights, smoking, stamping their feet against the cold, relieved that it is us, not them, trapped in the wreckage at the bottom of the hill.

When the ambulance arrives we are checked for broken bones and carefully extracted. They seem to spend a lot of time with Claire. A paramedic kneels beside me and puts a hand on my shoulder.

'Lucky,' he says in English.

'My girlfriend.' It hurts to talk. 'Claire. Is she okay?'

'Lucky,' he says again, grinning at me.

They carry me to the ambulance first. As the stretcher crests the hill the accident scene unfolds before me. Blue lights flash. Policemen wave curious motorists on with torches. White faces, open-mouthed, press against the windows of slow-moving cars. Ghouls, they trace the progress of my corpse towards the waiting ambulance. I turn my head away.

The horse lies still now, silhouetted by the headlights, steam rising from its haunches. A small cluster of men stand beside it. A policeman raises his foot and prods the beast with his toe. There is no movement. I feel a lump rise in my throat and then I am swallowed by the ambulance.

She is placed gingerly beside me. Red rags. Blood. Bandages. I cannot see her face. 'Claire?'

She does not respond. More muffled sobbing.

'Claire?'

I am aware of sirens, movement. Maybe I am in shock. Everything seems disjointed. The pain has started in my hand now. Deep. Throbbing. I try to move my fingers. I feel a grinding sensation and then I am violently ill. The paramedic leans over me again. 'You okay. You okay.' I try to move my hand again. This time the blackness comes.

*Simon told me, sincerely now it seems, 'Tell the ambulance to take you to . . . ' He paused, swaying, a finger in the air, Guinness perilously close to spilling.*

*'Tell the ambulance to take me?'*

*'Yes . . . Tell them . . . To the airport. Take you to the airport. Never. Never . . . ' He leaned close, conspirator, and belched. "Scuse me. Come here. Come here. Never let them get*

*you into one of their hospitals. Bastards.'*

*The expert. Veteran. Steeped in drink, we laughed. I should have listened.*

I woke up, violent. Violated. *Where the fuck . . . ? Oh Jesus.* A nurse came swimming into view, rushing towards me through treacle, keeping time with memory returning.

'Herr Dwyer. Herr Dwyer.'

Christ. A nightmare. No. Too real. All too real.

This is where they took us, Claire. Broken puppets, jarred and shaken. Broken bones and broken hearts. Mended, me. But you . . .

'Her injuries were so severe . . . ' A German doctor, neat moustache, wire glasses, narrow face. So young. 'Nothing we could do.'

Bastard. Nothing you could do? Bastard.

'Her spine, Mr Dwyer. I'm sorry. Her injuries were so severe . . . ' He splayed his hands, like a priest about to turn the water into wine. *Look. Nothing up my sleeves.* 'Nothing we could do.' He turned and left me lying with the sheet twisted in my good hand, staring out the window at German rain.

They let me see you. Sleeping. Could have been you. I couldn't tell. The bandages. Your breath rattled through ruined rhinal passages. I took your hand in mine, the good one, and held it, waiting for you to wake up, until I fell asleep, exhausted, and they took me to my room.

How many days, Claire? Repeated. You in a coma, me in a trance. And when you woke, bewildered and confused, I was the first one that you saw.

'Claire. Claire. It's okay. I'm here. It's me. Michael.'

'Michael?' The voice was not like yours. 'Where am I?'

'It's all right. It's all right.' But it was not all right.

Oh, Claire. The terror in your voice. Clutching at my hand when realisation struck. 'Michael. Oh my God. Michael. I can't move my legs. I can't . . . Oh, Michael.'

'Your spine, Claire . . . There was nothing they could do . . . '

I sat with you for hours, Claire. Days. Watched you staring at the mirror. Mummy. Black eyes against white bandages. Sinking deeper into your depression. I was powerless. *Nothing I could do.* At last, you turned to me, tortured, and made my blood run cold.

'I wish that I had died.'

There is a feeling of sameness. Inevitability. My life has become a series of endings. Naive youth, I used to wish my days away, waiting. For something to begin. Blind, I missed beginnings. And middles. Only endings capture my attention. Loss and I are never strangers.

Watery eyes behind bandages. A fist closes on my heart. She doesn't have to speak. I know what she will say. Predictable.

Her voice is thick, slurred since the accident. She finds it difficult to speak. I can hear the pain in her voice. What she has to say is not easy to hear at the best of times. Guilt? Multiplied.

'I swore I wouldn't let you hurt me this time.' Bitter.

'I didn't mean to.'

'I know. But you just can't help it, can you? If it's not emotional, it's physical. All beyond your control.'

All beyond my control. The airport hums around us. People bustling. Comings, goings. Smiles, tears. She looks small in the wheelchair. Broken. Swathed in bandages, like the invisible woman waiting to board.

'Will you be okay?' Idiot. Of course she won't.

'Oh sure, Michael. I love being a mummy.' A different pain. 'What do you want from me? Absolution?'

Uncomfortable. Yes, that is precisely what I want. I shift my weight and stare at the ground. 'I'm sorry, Claire.'

'Oh, for Christ's sake. If I hear that one more time . . . I know you're sorry. But that doesn't help, does it?' It is as if she is talking to a small boy.

'Listen. I want . . . I don't know what I want.' I squat down beside her and take her hand in mine. It feels cold, unresponsive. 'Claire. I'm here for you.'

As if that makes everything all right. As if that makes anything all right. There is a distance between us. I am speaking to myself.

'Claire?'

Her head turns slowly, deliberately, until she is looking straight into my eyes, unblinking.

'Michael. I don't want your pity. I don't want you. You've hurt me enough already.' Her words are steady. There is a quiet calmness about her. I can feel her slipping away from me.

'I'll never hurt you again. I swear.' I am genuine, desperate to atone. I want to make her understand that I love her. Now more than ever. She needs me. Somebody needs me.

'I'll never walk again, Michael. That's a fact. I'll never look in a mirror again without remembering. That's a fact. You *will* hurt me. If I let you. That, too, is a fact.' She pulls her hand away but her eyes remain fixed on mine.

'No, Claire. I won't. I . . . Won't . . .'

'Maybe not straight away. But think about it. You. The most selfish man I ever met. Can you see yourself being satisfied with a cripple for the rest of your life?' I cannot look into her eyes any more. I allow my gaze to wander, settling on a small child, tugging at her mother's arm, pointing at us, mouthing questions. 'No. It would only be a matter of time, Michael. Until the lies started. Until you started to feel trapped. We both know how you'd handle that, don't we? I can't depend on you. I won't depend on you. You would let me down, Michael, and that would kill me.'

She is right. I know it. I cannot deny it. I despise my weakness. Oh God, how I wish, though, for her to be wrong. Just this once, just this one time, let me be who I want to be. Let me be the good guy. Give me a chance. Let me prove myself. Let me prove *to* myself. *Give me a chance.* 'Give me a chance.'

'Let go, Michael. Give *me* a chance. At survival. I can't do this unless you let me go.'

I am crying. I can feel hot tears on my cheeks. 'Claire. Please.' I am clutching at her hand again. Begging.

'No. You wouldn't be doing it for me. You'd be doing it for you. That's a luxury I can't afford now.'

'Why don't you believe me? That's not how it would be.'

But maybe it is. Maybe I want her to salve my conscience. Maybe it is my need that drives, not hers. I realise that I don't even trust myself. She continues to look at me, pity in her eyes. She lifts her hand and touches me gently on the cheek, wiping away a tear. When her voice comes it is a whisper, like a prudent priest in the confessional.

'Let it go, Michael. It's all right to let it go.' *I absolve you of your sins.* I kneel beside her, head in her lap, sobbing, and she strokes the back of my head. Soft voice, soothing. 'It's all right. It's all right.'

Poor, injured soul. You, who have the greater need. Damaged. You comfort me. Me. Child. Freshy wakened from midnight screams. Mother's touch. Lover? No. No longer. Desire shattered with the windscreen. Wiped away. Devoured by ugly wounds. Subsumed by pain. What does that make me? Shallow? No. This goes deep. I love you, but everything is different now. Transformed. A different kind of love. A tragic love?

'Let me look after you.' Muffled. Speaking to the fabric of her jeans. Dead legs.

Her hand caresses the back of my neck. Slow, steady strokes. A sigh rattles through her ruined nose. 'No, Michael. Who'd look after you?'

And there it is.

Later, I sit in the departures lounge, surrounded by travellers, cradling my shattered left hand. Noise. Motion. Echoes of the accident. I am tired. Another traveller, tired of the journey. Claire understood me better than I understood myself. The pilgrimage continues. Footsore, world weary, alone. She set me free. Free to search.

'Who'd look after you?' Her words.

But I am so tired.

I stand, warily, feeling suddenly old. Her flight has vanished from the departures board. I dig my right hand deep into my jacket pocket and feel the rental car keys dig into my knuckles. I know I must go on. Another start. Another pilgrimage. Keep going. How?

'Oh sweet Christ.' A passing woman looks sharply at me, talking to myself, and gives me a wide berth. I grin at her. Reflex. Turning, I walk towards the car park.

I have learned, Claire. Your tragedy traps me. Haunts me. Sometimes, waking, time stops. I am held, motionless. Reflections of me in memory's mirror. Cold chills. Guilt. Grief.

There were things I could have, should have, told you too. Like my father. Lost. *He knew you loved him, Michael.* Pillow-talk. How did you know? How could he have known? *He knew.* Words of clichéd consolation for the contrite. You didn't know, Claire. Did you?

Last night I woke sweating. I saw you. Real. You walked, Claire. *Walked.* You spoke to me. You understood me. *It's not that you don't love, Michael, it's that you love too much.* My God, Claire, how beautiful you are in my vision. Oneiric oracle. Angel. The scars are gone.

And in my dream I see you coming home from the doctor's surgery. They flap around you, comforting, they think. *Hardly notice. Wonderful job. Good as new.* I can see your soul. Your injuries are deeper than they know. Wheeled to your room, you want to be alone. *Of course, darling.* Parents withdraw. *She'll be all right. Please God. In time. Give it time.* What time? Time is what you didn't have.

Alone, you took the pen I had given you for your twenty-first birthday from its place in the top drawer of your writing table. I see you run your fingers over the inscription, tiny scars scored in the metal. Braille, almost. A permanent testament to an undying love. Tears well in your eyes. Your hand moves to your face, fingers tracing the fine scars there. Permanent.

Through you I hear the television in the sitting-room. Your parents. Babysitters. It hurt you to move home. Another sacrifice. Independence. No choice. Cripple. Can't be left alone. *Alone.*

Your hand shakes as you write the note.

*Michael,*

    *The bandages came off today. It doesn't get any better than this.*

    *I love you,*

*Claire*

What more is there to say? You leave the note on the writing table, pure white rectangle, flimsy against dark solid oak. Black spider letters creep across the page. *Being of sound . . .* Nothing left, you leave nothing.

Your father has carefully arranged the bathroom. Everything within reach. This was once their room. En suite. *We don't need it, love. Sure, it'll be handy for you.* You realise that you still have the pen with you when you see it reflected in the medicine cabinet mirror, your own puzzled face strange to you in the background. First time you've seen the surgeon's handiwork. You drop the pen, absent-mindedly, into the glass beside your toothbrush and study your face in the mirror, again tracing the scars with your fingers. Remembering. 'Not my face,' you whisper to the stranger there, the image blurred by tears.

You open the medicine cabinet. Tabernacle. Through your

eyes I see the small brown bottle in its customary place. I can feel the pill on my tongue, relief washing over me, escape from the pain. Oh, Claire. The fear. The demons will return. You will wake in darkness, alone, rats gnawing at the raw flesh of your new face. No escape. The pills are an illusion. How could anyone understand?

I see you struggle from your wheelchair. Beads of perspiration on your brow, your arms were not made for this kind of exertion. You flop onto the bed, fish, useless legs dangling over the edge. You lie there, panting, staring at the ceiling. Trying to catch your breath. God damn. Why must everything be so hard?

Then you lift the phone from the bedside table and begin to enter my number, the white plastic smooth against your hand. With one number to go, you hesitate, finger hovering over the black button like a question mark. You sit like this, thinking, drifting, wondering what to say, what I will say, until the busy signal startles you. Replacing the receiver you turn your attention back to the bottle in your lap. You tip the blue and white capsules out onto the bedspread. You hold one between your thumb and forefinger, examining it. Small. Harmless. Your mother has left a glass of water on the bedside table for you. You pop the pill into your mouth and take a sip of water. One pill will not be enough. You know this. The pain will never really go away. There are so many kinds of pain. You take a second pill. And a third. And a fourth. Calmly, methodically, you continue to swallow the tablets until they are all gone. Then you pick up the phone again. This time you finish dialling my number.

'Michael? Are you there? Please pick up.'

My vision becomes juxtaposed with reality. Claire. I was there. I sat, hunched in the corner, in darkness, listening to your voice. Do you know that now? Is that why you haunt me? Did you think that your final conversation was with a machine, Claire? I was there. I heard you. God forgive me. I wanted to be alone. I did not want to talk to you. I was feeling sorry for myself. I had no idea how alone you were. I had no idea.

'Michael, I just . . . just wanted to hear your voice. I suppose a recording will have to do. I'm just . . . so . . . I don't know . . . I suppose I just wanted . . . wanted to say I'm sorry.' Your voice is small and frightened on the tape. I listen to it sometimes. Morbid? Maybe. It's all that I have left of you. It reminds me. I hear your words fade, your breathing grow more shallow. You do not hang up, you lie there with the phone pressed to your lips. *I love you, Michael Dwyer.* Last words. Alone. Talking to a machine. You fall asleep. You never wake up.

*Dear Maria,*

*Another letter I will never send. Unbeknownst to you, you have become my confidante. What would I do without you? Intimate scrawl crawls across a page, spilling pain. Inkblots on paper. Words written and hidden. Neat bundles, bottom drawer. Like letters from a lover. Letters to a lover. The written word has become my confessional, Maria. A time to face my sins. Picture this, tortured scribe, craving absolution. Bless me, father, undersigned.*

*Who else can I turn to? Former lover, mother of my child. Soul mate. Nobody knows me like you do, nobody cares the way you can. Would you mourn me, Maria? If I died tonight? Would you? I know, I know. If I spoke these words to you, you would laugh in my face. 'Cop yourself on, Dwyer.' I can hear you speak the words. But, oh, Maria, I feel so alone. I am so ashamed.*

*Perhaps you saw the newspaper. You may have thought, in passing, 'Poor thing!' But had you read between the lines, you may have lingered, finger poised above the page, thinking. Had you known it all. You had so much in common, you two. You would have understood. Maybe.*

*Claire is gone now, Maria. No. Not gone. How could she be gone? She is still here, haunting. Dead. That's the word. Simple. There is no nice way to say it. Suicide? No. That's not right either. It would be inaccurate to say she took her life. That honour lies with me. I took her life, Maria. Me. She merely chose an end to suffering. Can you blame her, Maria? Can you? And what does that make me? Murderer? Surely. As if I forced the tablets into her mouth and pushed them down her throat.*

*Christ, Maria. I burn with guilt. It consumes me, claws at my oesophagus until I cannot breathe. Michael's penance. Never rest. Waking. Sleeping. All the same. I can find no peace.*

*Of course, my rationale speaks soothing words, 'It's not my fault. Accidents happen.' But it isn't just for her, Maria. God, as if that weren't enough. I have caused such pain. And I've been careful in my life. Elusive. Too clever to transgress. It means nothing. It's not the things I did, Maria. My sins are sins of omission. The things I failed to do. Nobody knows that better than you.*

*I have spent a lifetime avoiding obstacles. Ostrich. Never make eye contact. If they can't catch you, they can't hurt you. But what disarray I have left in my path. Temporal turbulence, callously conscious of the casualties I cause. How can I plead innocence now? I could beg forgiveness, but this stigma stings. I could never forgive myself. That is where the true irony lies. I cannot run from myself. And underneath it all, Maria, when all the chips are down, I'm not really the bastard everybody thinks I am. I do feel. Too much. And that has been my downfall.*

*Another letter I will never send. Another futile explanation. Who am I trying to fool, Maria? I'll keep this with the others. Maybe someday I will show it to you. Maybe then you will understand the piece of me that lies hidden, even from you. Maybe then you will help me find salvation and the pilgrimage will end.*

*My love, as always,*

*Michael*

They would not have told me. My fault. I didn't really blame them. Gerry read about it in the *People* newspaper. Front page, her picture caught his eye in Easons. *Tragedy of Local Girl's Despair.* I missed the funeral. Unawares, Crosstown swallowed another piece of me. I am in danger of disappearing.

It was a week before I called to their door. Her father stood poised in the doorway, fists balled, a nerve twitching in his jaw. He is a small man, five foot two, maybe. I was afraid. I looked into his steady, red-ringed eyes and saw the hatred burn there.

'Mr Roche, I . . .'

Words refused to come. His wife appeared behind him. She put a hand on his arm. 'Brendan.' Soft voice. Gentle touch. The danger drained from him. I saw his shoulders sag, his jaw slacken.

'You're not welcome here.' The words burned him. He began to close the door in my face. I stuck out a hand to stop it.

'Wait. Please.'

He did not look at me. He stood, shoulder at the door, staring at the pattern on his hall carpet. 'I don't trust myself to talk to you, young man.' He seemed to spit the words like spoiled food through his dentures.

'Brendan,' his wife's voice again, as if speaking to a damaged child. 'Let him in.'

He turned on her, anger spilling from him, 'You do as you please.' He stamped past her into the bowels of the house. She raised her eyes to me, *Claire's eyes,* and smiled weakly.

'You'll have to excuse Brendan, Mr Dwyer. He isn't taking it very well. Come in to the kitchen.' She swung the door open and stood back to let me pass. I saw the sodden handkerchief wrapped around her knuckles and my heart broke all over again. Brave, beautiful woman.

I sat at the kitchen table, watching her make tea. Comfort

in the familiar. Solid ground. My own mother months before. The loss of a loved one. Resort to what you know.

'Do you take sugar?'

'No. Thanks.'

She poured milk into a jug and placed it in front of me, then rattled around in the cutlery drawer.

'Are you hungry? Will you have a sandwich? I was just going to make one for Brendan.'

'No. Really, I . . . Listen. There are some things I need to say.'

She stopped, hands buried in the drawer, facing away from me. I could see her shoulders shaking. She turned slowly to face me. When she spoke, her words were strained, she struggled for composure. 'What, Mr Dwyer? What do you need to say to me? I don't know why you came here. It can't have been easy for you, so I'm trying to be civil. But what do you possibly think you can say to me?'

'I . . . I loved her too.' Thin. Threadbare. I had nothing to offer this woman. I took her daughter. Flesh and blood. Nothing could compare. She stood, regarding me, dubious, head to one side, like her daughter used to do. *I know you, Michael Dwyer. I know your sort. You don't love anyone but yourself.* I heard the words. I blinked, stunned, formulating my response, before I realised that she had not spoken. The only sound was the kettle, coming to the boil. She was waiting. Waiting for something more. 'I just . . . loved her.'

She sighed, bread-knife hanging loosely in her hand. I wished she would plunge it into my heart. I could see her hands, slick with arterial blood, maternal face, twisted in anger, plastic teeth exposed. I lay Christlike on the floor, arms extended. *My life for hers.*

The kettle snapped off, jerking me back to reality. She turned to her chore, resigned. 'When you left, the last time, it broke her heart. I know. I was left to pick up the pieces. It was beyond even me this time.' She was gentle, wistful. She looked at me over her shoulder as she poured the water onto the tea-leaves. 'Why did you have to come back?'

'I don't know.' I began to realise the mistake that I was making. I should have left these people alone. I could not ease their pain. I had known that, really. Maybe I thought that they could ease mine.

'I heard you have a child.'

'A little girl, yes. News travels fast.'

'Wexford is a small place.'

'Yes.'

'Michael,' she hesitated. 'Can I call you Michael?' *Imagine asking.* I nodded. 'I'll pray for you. That you never have to feel what Brendan and I are feeling now. You had no business being with Claire, Michael. And she had no business being with you. Now stop all this codology and go to your child. That's where you should have been in the first place.'

I watched her pouring the tea into a white mug. She handed it to me. 'Are you sure you won't have a sandwich?'

'Yeah. Thanks.'

'Drink your tea. I'll be back in a minute.'

She left me alone with my thoughts. I sipped the tea, waiting for her. I could hear her talking to her husband in the living-room, snippets of their conversation, his voice raised and angry, her trying to calm him down. *What does he want? Get him out of this house. Now ,Brendan. Ah Brendan me arse.* One word rang across my brain: *Forgive.*

When she returned to the kitchen she smiled at me apologetically. She settled in a chair opposite me at the table. 'Is the tea all right?'

'Lovely, thanks.' I looked at my hands, wrapped around the mug. 'Look. Mrs Roche, I don't know what to say to you. I didn't mean to upset your husband. I don't even know why I'm here, really. It just . . . It just seemed like the right thing to do. You know?'

She just sat looking at me.

'Listen, thanks for the tea.' I stood up. 'I think I'd better be going. Please tell Mr Roche . . . I don't know. Tell him I'm sorry.'

She stood too. 'Okay, Michael. I will.' She smiled at me and touched my hand. 'Come on. I'll show you out.'

In the hallway, I saw Brendan Roche staring at me from the living-room. Our eyes met. The hatred had returned to his. I nodded and turned towards the front door.

Mrs Roche stood huddled on the doorstep, arms wrapped around herself against the cold. 'My daughter loved you, Michael. I don't know if I should do this, but here.' She handed me a brown envelope. 'Goodbye, Michael.'

'Goodbye, Mrs Roche. I truly am sorry.'

'I know. I know.' She stepped inside and closed the door.

I sat in the car and opened the envelope. It contained a photograph, a pen, and a white slip of paper, folded in two. The photograph was taken at my graduation ball. She is dressed in green, her brown hair tied back, wearing her mother's pearls. She is so young. So happy. So beautiful. Her writing on the back of the photograph. *Michael's grad. 1/3/'81. It doesn't get any better than this.* I gave her the pen for her twenty-first birthday. Silver. Engraved. I unfolded the paper. Her handwriting.

*Michael,*
*The bandages came off today. It doesn't get any better than this.*

*I love you,*

*Claire*

# As It Was in the Beginning

There is a recurring theme to my thoughts. An echo, straining, like a fractured melody, maddeningly familiar. Twisted notes, elusive, dangling. A haunting.

Memories taunt me. Our father, who art in Heaven until the hour of my death. Daddy-long-legs. Long. Legs. Dead. Fractured face. Murderer. She is there. Constantly. *Think you're free?* She reels me in. Fisherwoman. *By the way Michael, fuck you.* Fishwife. *Wife?* Father's wife. Mother. Guilt. Old woman. *'I can't come back.'* *'Nobody asked you.'* I strain against that line, proud fish. Hooks bite. Barbed. Dig deep. Struggle. Dragged by searing snare, escape escapes me.

Frank sounds confused. *Speak up. I can't hear you.* Another one of age's associates. Assaulted through the years. Ears, Frank. Failing. Treacherous toads. It seems you can't depend on anyone. Least of all yourself.

'It's Michael, Frank.' My patience wearing thin. Perhaps I should just hang up and leave him cursing at young pups making obscene phone calls.

'What? Who?' He shouts into the phone, as if I am the deaf one.

'Michael,' I scream. 'Michael Dwyer.'

'Oh, Michael. Jaysus. Howarya, hun? Where are you?'

'Germany.'

'Germany?' Incredulous. The dark side of the moon. 'Jaysus. Isn't that great? You're in Germany, are you?'

'Yeah. Germany. Listen . . .'

'How are ya keepin', Michael?'

'Fine, Frank. I'm fine. Listen, I can't chat. The phone bill. You know? I'm trying to contact my mother. She hasn't been answering her phone. You don't know where she is, do you?'

There is silence on the line, a vague electronic hum.

'Frank?'

'Oh Jesus, hun. Your mammy is in hospital. In Dublin. Did no one tell you?'

No, Frank. Nobody told me. Not even her. Now I am silent. My turn to be confused. As if I deserve the benefit of anybody's doubt.

Jonathan Witherspoon looks at me evenly over steepled surgeon's fingers, his watery eyes afloat behind milk-bottle lenses. Goldfish. He is a grey man, almost completely bald. A fine dusting of hair runs in a semicircle around his head, just above the ears. Grey hair, grey head. Concrete cranium. He wears a moustache. Pencil thin, pencil grey. He is a gaunt man. 'Looks delicate,' as my mother would say. His long fingers reach up to unwind his wire-rimmed spectacles. Beady eyes blinking incessantly, he is a tortoise, pulled from his shell in broad, bright daylight. He does not look like a doctor now. I watch him breathe on the lenses, fine fog spreading on the glass, in his hand a pristine handkerchief, plucked from a pocket. Conjuror. My eyes follow his thumb, gently rubbing at the glass with the white starched cloth. I am vaguely aware that he is clearing his throat. I am preoccupied by his small, deliberate actions, so much so that his words do not register at first. It takes a moment to realise that he has spoken.

'Your mother is not a well woman, Mr Dwyer. The cancer is widespread and, frankly, I feel that surgery would not improve matters.'

When I look at him, he is replacing his spectacles. He extends a bony finger and settles them on his nose, peering through the glass at me, his barrier restored. *Is this how you always deliver the bad news? De-spectacled intimacy?* He folds his arms on the desktop in front of him, leaning towards me. Business as usual.

'Oh.'

He regards me for a moment longer, as if expecting something more. What is there to say? He unfolds his arms and starts to straighten papers on his desk. Suddenly I do not deserve his full attention.

'Of course, we will do everything in our power to make her as comfortable as possible, but I do have to inform you that her situation is . . . '

'How long?'

'I beg your pardon?' He stops, hand poised in midair, full of papers being transferred from one tray to another. In. Out. *Shake it all about.* I cannot help it. The thought sticks to me like chocolate, stubborn stain. I can see him looking at the smile on my lips. What must he be thinking?

'I'm sorry, Doctor. I mean, how long does my mother have?'

He hesitates, reluctant, unsure of me. 'Not very long, I'm afraid. A couple of weeks. No more.'

There is a stillness in the room. I sit quietly. Thinking.

'Have you told her?'

He seems relieved that it is me who breaks the silence. Words gush. 'Oh yes, she's known for quite some time.'

Secret. How it must have burned. This thing growing inside her. Why didn't she tell me? Why should she? I have taught her not to depend on me.

'Are you all right, Mr Dwyer?'

'Michael.'

'Sorry?'

'Mr Dwyer was my father.'

'Oh. Yes. Of course, Mr . . . Michael. Um . . . Are you?'

'What?'

'All right.'

Strangers. We are thrown together. We do not understand each other. I am not this man's friend and he is not mine. His concern is merely professional courtesy. Why should it be any different? I am just another relative. One of the crowd. He will forget me as soon as I leave the office. How many sons, daughters, brothers, sisters, husbands, wives have been in this chair? How many lives shattered? *Comfort me, Doctor. Comfort me.* Oh, but I am different, Doctor. Traveller. Cold. It can't hurt if you don't care. Can it?

He is looking at me. Waiting for an answer. Fuck you. I will not be ordinary. I will not let you see my pain. *If you want to see my heart break, you'll need a scalpel, boy.* I meet his eye. Hostile. Aggressor. I can see that he is taken aback, confused, perhaps even a little frightened. But there is no satisfaction in it for me.

'I want to see her.'

'Yes. Yes. Of course you do.'

Sterile, antiseptic. Nurse heels click in cold corridors. Old woman. Withered. Blue veins criss-cross white stretched skin. Marble mother. Kept alive by tubes and things. Mechanical, regular breathing forcing tired lungs. I take her hand. Eyelids flutter, birdlike. 'Mammy. I'm here now.' Here. Now. Conscience creeps chestward. Squeezes. Worm. Yeah. Now, maybe. Green pulse, heartbeat pointing. You. You. You.

There is a sound in her throat. 'Don't try to speak, Mammy. I'm here. Shush.'

She fixes a watery eye on me, holding me with her gaze. Accusatory? If she could speak, what would she say? Would she pour her heart out? *Where were you, son? I have been so afraid. I needed you.* No. Probably not. She would not blame me. She never has, really. Michael can do no wrong. She would probably joke with me, pretend that everything was all right. Trivialise. *Did you see Sparrowfart? What kind of a name is Witherspoon? Sure, God spoke before them all.* And what would I do, penitent son? Would I whip myself into a frenzy? *Oh my God, Mother, you're going to die and I love you so much and I should have been here for you and I should . . .* No. I would hide behind your strength. I would pretend, like I always do, that I had done no wrong. You know it, Mother. I know it. I have wronged you. But it is left unspoken. From no care at all to intensive care. Too little, too late. I sit holding your hand.

'It's going to be all right, Mammy. I'm here now.'

But nothing is all right.

She wakes, a ghost come fleetingly to bid adieu. Old woman, tongue-tied. Like me, as a child, forcing words to lodge against lazy lips. Struggle. Bulging eyes. Intelligence inhabiting a husk. *Take the tube out. For a moment. Let me hear my mother speak her mind.*

'A moment, Mr Dwyer. No more. She's very weak.' Matron pauses, hand left lightly on my shoulder. Squeezes. Then she is gone, dissolving down the ward like Spock transported. Now we are alone. Except for the heart transplant in the next bed.

'You knew, Ma. Didn't you? Why didn't you tell me?' The colour is gone from her. A grey thing, she swallows, and gasps against the pain. I wish that I could help. Her hand is cold in mine, as if she is already dead, a limp thing, like a Christian Brother I once knew.

'Michael.' One word. Toad croak. A single word, and yet it says so much. There is still time.

'Oh, Ma. It's all right. Don't try to speak, Ma. I'm here. I'm here.'

Listen to me. *Ma*. She would have given me a clip across the ear for that when I was younger. *What do you think we are? Sheep?* A flick of the tea towel maybe, smiling. When she was stronger. Before the cancer came.

'Christ, Ma. Cancer. You knew. Last Christmas. I left you alone. Why didn't you tell me? Why didn't you say?'

And if she had the strength, perhaps she'd ask me if it would have made a difference. Would I have come? And why? To watch an old woman wither? *'No need,' she would say, perhaps. 'It will all be yours when I'm gone anyway. I have nobody else. Not even Sarah. You made sure of that.'*

And what if I had gone? Would it have helped? Truculent, we would sit together, silent, after turkey. Watching *Gone with the Wind* again. Every now and then she would fix me with a baleful glare and spit an accusation from her chair beside the fire. Like coal. Crackling. *Your father never got over you going away.* Like I killed him. Like it was my fault, Mother. Everything was always my fault. Like monuments we'd sit there, me counting the minutes until my escape. St Stephen's Day. An early train . . .

But maybe it would have been different. New friendship forged. Sitting on the floor with a bottle of wine between us, looking at old photo albums of when I was small.

*'Look how happy your father was.'*

'*Who's that?*'

'*Your great aunt Alice.*'

We would have laughed and opened presents by the fire.

'*A sock. How sweet.*'

'*You'll get the other one tomorrow. I wanted to make sure you'd stay.*'

'*Touché.*'

And kissing her goodnight, I might have climbed the stairs and sunk into my childhood bed with pleasant thoughts of Santa Claus and midnight Mass gone by. 'Tomorrow,' I might have said, my face against the pillow. 'Tomorrow I'll call Maria. Maybe we can start again.' Nativity.

Too late. I didn't go. Instead I sat alone, half drunk, listening to merriment drifting from the flat below.

'*Herr Dwyer, come and join us.*'

'*No. Thanks. I think I have a cold.*'

And she was left to nurse her secret silently. Merry Christmas, Mother, mourning still. Blood in the toilet bowl. Crimson. Christmas. Future?

'Michael.' She is pulling at my hand. I lean close.

'Lie still, Ma. Easy.' She's struggling to speak. 'Shh. It's okay. Every . . .'

'Michael.' The tendons strain in her neck as she struggles to lift her head, to look around.

'Yeah. I'm here, Ma,' I whisper. 'I came. I'm here now. Everything's going to be all right. I love you, Ma. You know that, don't you? Love you. I never told Daddy, never got the chance, but I loved him too. Oh, Ma. You should have told me. Should have . . .'

'Michael.' Poor old dear. I push her back, gently, on the pillow.

'Yeah, Ma. Yeah. I'm here. I came.' In time. Thank God.

'Where's Michael?'

I am stunned. Then she is gone, slipping back to sleep, and I am left holding her hand, helpless, surrounded by electronic beeps and liquid crystal.

Gerry found me in the waiting-room, sipping cold coffee from a plastic cup, awash in a sea of human misery. 'Are you all right, Michael?' Give me a definition and I'll tell you.

Waiting is the worst. So much suffering. I am unable to hide. I am naked and alone. Exposed. Vulnerable. They stab me with their stories.

The woman on my left bore six children. She is alone here, waiting for her husband to die. 'They're all in England now,' she tells me, conspiratorial whisper cutting through the semi-silence of shuffling feet and cleared throats. 'They'll be here tomorrow.' She pauses, shifting her purse in her lap, blinking. Soft grey eyes, red-rimmed. She is pale, drawn. 'Well, maybe not Seamus. He might not be able to get the time off work. But the others. They'll be here tomorrow.' Poor soul. Yes. Here tomorrow. Too late. They'll stay for the funeral and then they'll be gone. Back to England. I know.

The man on my right waits for news of his eldest son, stabbed last night in a brawl outside a city-centre pub. Critical condition. He sits in silence, elbows on his knees, hands clasped, head bowed. He prays quietly, no tears left to cry. He lost his only other son last year. A BMW and a brick wall. He had to identify the body. Badly burned. Baby. Senseless. Sixteen years old. Joyrider.

The list is endless. I sit among them, soon to be orphan, listening. *Nice young man.* I am filled with pity for them. I feel their pain. Real. Sucking the marrow from their bones, chewing at their eyeballs. But there is a distance between us. I can sympathise, but I cannot be one of them. I have developed an immunity. I am numb. There are no surprises for me now. I have learned to accept the inevitable.

Gerry put a hand on my shoulder. Concerned. 'Have you eaten?'

'Yeah, thanks. I had a sandwich in the cafeteria about an hour ago.'

'Just a sandwich?'

'No. I had a packet of crisps too. Cheese and onion. You

174

can't get them in Germany. Or sliced pan. Did I ever tell you that?'

'Michael, you're rambling.' He looked at me steadily. 'You need to get out of here for a while. Come on. I'll buy you a pint. I think there's a pub on the corner.'

'We're in Ireland, Gerry. There's a pub on every corner.'

The sun shone weakly down Eccles Street as we left the hospital, making me squint. The sunlight seemed incongruous. I pulled my coat around me, hands dug deep in the pockets, and shivered. 'What time is it?'

Gerry glanced at his watch. 'About five.'

'Shouldn't you be at work?'

'It's Saturday.'

'Oh.'

'Come on. Let's get inside. It's fuckin' freezin' out here.' He led me across the street and into the pub. Inside was disturbingly normal, the smell of the beer, the sound of talk and laughter, glasses clinking behind the bar. I stood in the doorway, surveying the scene before me. Pockets of people. Warm. Comfortable. Happy. Barmen in white shirts, gathering glasses. A blonde woman with too much lipstick, head thrown back, mouth wide with laughter, clutching a clear drink with one hand and a young man's knee with the other. My mother lay dying, feet from here. Inconsequential, trivial. These people went about their business, oblivious to the unfolding misery mere paces away.

Gerry indicated an empty table. 'Grab that. What'll you have?'

I shook myself. *Wake up, Dwyer.* 'Smithwicks.'

'Guinness head?'

'Yeah.'

He handed me his coat and headed for the bar.

I sat at the table and picked up a beer-mat, absent-mindedly tearing strips off it and dropping them into the ashtray. I saw an elderly man sitting on his own at the bar with a pint of Guinness and a whiskey chaser. I recognised him from the hospital. He looked at me, expressionless, and nodded. His wife had been in the same ward as my mother. Heart attack. She died that morning. It seems that, no matter how inconspicuous, tragedy is never far away. I nodded back. Solemn. He turned back to his Guinness, his whiskey and his own reflection in the mirror behind the bar.

Gerry came towards me with two pints and a packet of crisps. He straddled the stool opposite me. 'Seeing as you can't get these in Germany,' he said, handing me the crisps.

'Cheers, mate,' I said, taking a pint from him. 'You could be shot for this too,' I told him, raising the tattered beer-mat. 'Do you remember the *Deckel* system?'

'Oh yeah. You don't pay for your drinks until the end of the night. Weird.'

'I've always thought it was strange, all right. Ticking off your drinks on a beer-mat. It'd never work in Ireland. People are always tearing them up. They say it's a sign of sexual frustration.'

Gerry looked at the pile of shredded paper in the ashtray. 'You tell me.'

I grinned, despite myself.

Gerry raised his pint to me. 'Cheers.' He drank deeply, eyes closed, and then lowered his pint, smacking his lips. 'Jaysus, I needed that.' I sipped at my own pint. Silent. He took a packet of cigarettes from his pocket and started to unwrap them.

'When did you start smoking again?' I asked.

'I didn't. For fuck's sake don't tell Eileen. She's still off them. We have a bet.' *Another bet.* He lit a cigarette and took a drag, blowing smoke back through his nose. 'How's your ma doing?'

'Unconscious. Just woke up for a while, then slipped back. I'll tell you, mate, I'm starting to get very sick of hospitals.'

'Claire?'

'Yeah. Jesus. Is there no end to it? Christ, Gerry. She

doesn't even know I'm here.'

'It's tough all right. Is there anything we can do, Michael? Me and Eileen?'

'No. Nothing anyone can do, really.' I smiled, ironically. 'Pray, maybe. That's what she'd say.'

'We already are praying, Michael.' I looked at him sharply, thinking he was mocking me, but he was serious.

'Thanks.' He waved a hand, dismissive. The end of his cigarette flared minutely. 'Jesus, Gerry. So many people are leaving me. My father. Claire. Now this. I don't mind telling you, I'm beginning to feel a little bit insecure.'

'Don't start feeling sorry for yourself, Michael. Worst thing you can do.'

'Yeah. I know.'

We sat quietly for a minute, sipping our pints, listening to the hum of the pub. I saw the old man from the hospital order another Guinness. He counted coins out on the bar beside his cap, a drop of snot hanging from his red nose. The barman stood, impatient, hand extended. I imagined his foot tap-tapping behind the bar. *Come on, you silly old fart.* Patience. Gerry followed my gaze, wondering.

'So. Have you spoken to Maria?'

'No.'

'You should call her, you know. She'd want to know.' He picked at something on the tip of his tongue and tapped ash into the ashtray.

'Yeah, I suppose.'

'When was the last time you saw her?'

'I don't know. Good while ago.' *By the way, Michael. Fuck you.* 'I don't think she'd want to see me.'

'Eileen thinks she would.'

'Eileen would. Last of the great romantics. No. Face it, Gerry. Some things just aren't meant to be.'

'Bullshit. I think you're afraid, Dwyer.' He looked meaningfully at me.

'No. No . . . It's not that . . . It's just . . . Well. The last time I saw her, we talked about it and . . . Well, it just wasn't meant to be.'

He took another sip from his drink. 'Why not?'

'Well, for a start she asked me to move back home.'

'And?'

'What do you mean, "and"?'

'"And". I mean "and". Fucking "and". Okay?' He dragged on his cigarette, took another drink and banged his glass down on the table, smiling to himself. 'Jesus Christ, it's like trying to get blood from a stone.'

'*And* I didn't want to, okay?'

'Why not? For Christ's sake, Michael. Are you mad? If she was prepared to give you another chance . . . I mean . . . With the baby and all . . . Jesus Christ, man.'

I noticed that his pint was nearly gone. I had hardly touched mine. I was not used to drinking like an Irishman any more. I raised the glass to my lips. 'I just wasn't ready.' I gulped down some of the red-brown liquid.

'Are you ready now?'

'I don't know, Gerry. I honestly don't know.'

Gerry sighed. 'Michael, let me tell you something. You'll never be ready. When Paul was born I thought I'd die. I had panic attacks every time I thought about it. I mean, think about it. Me. Nappies. Bottles. Fucking swings and round-abouts, for fuck's sake. But you get used to it, Michael. Life's rich pattern and all that. You know?'

'Yeah. I know. Look. That's fine and all, Gerry, but I don't want to come back here. I think . . . Christ, I don't know what I think.'

'There's nothing wrong with here, Michael. In fact, there's a lot right with here. With Maria. With Sarah.' He blew smoke across the table at me. 'What's so great about Germany anyway? Seems to me you're always complaining about it.'

'Well there's the job, for starters.'

'There are jobs here.'

'I know. Look . . . This sounds silly, I know, but . . . Look, when I went to Germany it was on a kind of pilgrimage. I suppose if I was American I'd say that I was trying to find myself or something. But the pilgrimage never ended, Gerry. I suppose I never found what I was looking for.'

He laughed. 'Jesus Christ, Michael. Grow up, will you? Never found what you were looking for? Who do you think you are? Bono? I've got news for you, me auld flower. Nobody ever finds what they're looking for. Pilgrimage me bollox. What if Maria and Sarah are exactly what you're looking for? What if you're just too fucking stupid to see what's right in front of your nose?'

I was suddenly annoyed. Perhaps at him, perhaps at myself. He was trivialising my quest, my voyage of discovery. For years Gerry Hart had represented everything that I despised about my native land. He was docile, accepting, a bumpkin who could never understand the nobility, the sacrifice of the Irish Diaspora. Now I wanted to shout at him. *Stew in your own ignorance, Gerry. Congeal in the commonplace. Merge with the mediocre.*

But I knew that he was right. That everything I needed had been right in front of me the whole time. And knowing that was more than I could bear. The loss of my father, a man I should have known. Claire. Gone because of me, pathetic pilgrim. Her mother's words. *You had no business.* My shrunken mother, cancer-ridden, alone. Loath to tell her only living relative about the disease devouring her. He was right. Time to grow up. But I also knew that it was all too late for me. *There's no going back, Michael. Nobody to go back to.*

'Look,' I said, 'I don't expect you to understand. You have everything you want, Gerry. A wife. A family. Security. You know what you want. Who you are. It's not like that for me. I've never been prepared to settle for a normal job, a normal house, a station wagon and two point five children. I've always wanted more.'

He watched me through heavy eyelids, mouth half-open, pondering his response. 'Michael, do you know what your problem is? You've got a serious case of God complex. There's nothing wrong with normal. Jesus, you're so full of it. Don't worry, though. It's easily cured. I'll just take you outside and kick the living shit out of you.'

I ran my finger down the outside of my pint glass, staring into the liquid, regretting having wanted to be better than him, my peer, my only friend. I took a deep breath, holding it, feeling it fill my lungs, then exhaled slowly. I looked at him, a chastened smile on my lips. 'I didn't mean to offend you, Gerry. That's not what I meant at all. You have a great life. You're a lucky man. Luckier than I'll ever be.'

'Bullshit,' he hissed at me. 'Horse manure, Michael. There you go again. Will you stop patronising me, for fuck's sake.'

'Christ, Gerry. I'm trying here. Give me a chance, for cryin' out loud. I only meant that you're lucky.'

'Luck has nothing to do with it, Michael. Take your head out of your arse. The only difference between you and me is that I have sense. At least sense enough to listen to Eileen. You have a wife and family too, only you're too thick-headed to realise it.' He dug around in his jeans pocket and pulled out a fifty-pence piece. He leaned across the table and pushed it into my hand. 'Here. Call Maria, you gobshite. Before it's too late.' He drained the last of his pint and stubbed out his cigarette in the ashtray, glowering at me. 'And get me another fucking pint while you're at it.'

I bought him his pint, but I did not call Maria. I knew that Gerry was right about a lot of things, but when it came to Maria, I believed that it was already too late.

When I got back to the hospital I knocked softly on the door to the intensive care unit. One of the nurses came to the door. Kitty. Her face dropped when she saw me. I knew immediately.

'Oh, Mr Dwyer,' she said, putting her hand on my arm, concern written all over her face. 'Come and sit down.' She led me up the corridor and sat beside me on a window ledge. I could smell the soap on her skin. She leaned close to me, taking my hand. Angel of mercy. Young. So young. Pink face framed by golden hair. White starched uniform. 'I'm so sorry,' she massaged my hand with both of hers, looking earnestly into my eyes. 'Mr Dwyer. Michael.' She paused. 'I'm afraid your mother passed away about half an hour ago.'

# WORLD WITHOUT END

Cold, blue, autumn sky. The earth yawns, gaping grave, beneath its blanket of leaves. Icy fingers of granite point at the sky. Brittle bones, touch them, they will splinter. Breath visible, black clothes. Crisp crunch of grey grass under black leather. The coffin looks small and worn out. Like her before she died. Dull brown, brass handles, swallowed whole. Father. You did not have to wait too long. She will lie beside you tonight. Welcome home, lover. A decade of the rosary. Glorious. Mystery. *Michael, I can see you. Head bowed. Sorrow. Tears for her or tears for you? Tears. All gone. Orphan. Only child. You are alone.* I am alone.

Maria came. She stood across the grave from me with Sarah in her arms. I walked her to her car. I carried our child, Maria at my elbow.

'Come back to the house for something to eat.'

'No, Michael, I don't think that's a good idea.'

'I miss you.'

'I know.'

We were standing by her car. Sarah twisted, reaching for my nose. I shifted her weight, sparrow, and gathered her doll's coat around her. She took my finger in a tiny, mitten-clad hand. I didn't want to let her go, but bent and helped Maria buckle her into her baby-seat. We straightened and stood there, awkward.

'Maria . . .'

'Don't.' Quick. A warning.

'What?' I sound exasperated. 'You don't even know what

182

I'm going to say.'

She snorts. 'I do. Don't waste your breath. It's over, Michael.'

'Just hear me out. Please?'

'Michael.' Her voice is low and hard. 'I don't want to fight with you at your mother's funeral. Can't this wait?'

'No, Maria. I'm drowning here. I need to make things right. Christ, I know I've been an asshole, but . . . Give me a chance, will you?'

She looked away from me, back across Wexford Harbour at the twin steeples, grey against the clear blue sky. 'No.' Soft, almost inaudible, a breath of wind.

'Maria, for what it's worth, I love you.'

She turned back to me, tears in her eyes, and touched my face, the black leather of her glove keeping any intimacy at bay. 'Maybe you do, Michael. Bury your mother. This is not the time or the place for this conversation.'

'Please . . . '

'No, Michael. Go home, will you?'

She climbed into the car. I held the door as she fastened her seat-belt.

'Maria. I . . . '

'Just close the bloody door, Michael.' Anger spilling out now. 'I can't talk to you like this. Not here. Not now.'

I hesitated, not wanting her to leave like this, but she pulled the door shut and put the car into gear. I took a step backwards and watched her drive out of the car park, then turned and walked towards a huddled group of mourners.

The house concealed a lifetime half forgotten. Every corner contained its own memory, struggling to the surface, jostling for my attention. Three lifetimes, lived between these walls. What are little boys made of? I would find a book my mother read to me, a stain on a carpet from something I once spilled. There, on the television, a trophy, kept by proud parents. My father's slippers still skulked beneath the couch, his robe carefully folded over a chair at the foot of her bed. She had never let him go. She waited a respectable eternity. For my sake? Then she followed him.

At first I thought that I could be ruthless. Throw it all away. Like Claire said, 'travel light'. Then I wanted to keep everything. I reopened boxes already nailed shut and re-examined relics previously condemned. Tea-chests piled around me, I sat on the floor. I cried. I laughed. I let my parents die.

I plucked a picture from the piano. A photograph in a silver frame. He is smiling at the camera. She is looking at him. Satisfied. Proud. *This is my husband.* Black and white. It was how I wanted to remember them. Black and white.

I ran the tap in the kitchen for a minute or two, looking out the window at her garden. I filled a glass and sat at the table, balancing my chair on two legs. She used to hate that. *Michael, will you sit down properly? You'll kill yourself one of these days, child of grace.* I drank, slowly, feeling the ice-cold water seep into my chest. The clock ticked. It was me who killed the cuckoo. I used to hate the bastard. Interrupting my peace when I came home late and sat here eating cheddar cheese sandwiches with too much mustard. I looked at the radiator where the fireplace used to be. I would stoke that fire when I came in, perished from my walk from town, more than likely soaked to the skin. She would stick her head around the door sooner or later. *Go to bed, child. Are you staying up all night to see if you snore?* She told me once that she would lie awake, praying for me, until she heard me close the door to my room at night. She couldn't sleep until she knew that I was safe. Poor Ma. What did she ever do to deserve me? I drained my glass, rinsed it, wrapped it in kitchen roll and put it in a waiting cardboard box.

It was dark at six o'clock. I turned on every light in the house. They had been methodical, careful to turn off every light behind them as they moved from room to room. Giant fireflies, lighting their immediate surroundings. Low wattage, scornful of the wastefulness of youth.

I sat on a naked bed and removed a lampshade, missed on my first manoeuvre. This room was mine. Still cold. Damp mattress. Childhood colds lurked here, waiting for me to return. The man, the passing pilgrim. *Take me with you. Let me share your sweaty bed, toss and turn all night with you beneath clinging sheets.* They never failed to make the trip back with me. Running. Nose.

I undressed the house. Unhurried. Passion hidden deep. Contained. Running a finger along a curve that took my eye, pausing to ponder old areas recently remembered. I exposed it piece by piece. Slow, tantalising. Wait here. Linger. Look there. White patches appearing as layers were peeled away. And when, eventually, it stood before me, stripped of all its trappings, it looked like any other house. Bricks, mortar, floors, ceilings. Shell.

They came and took everything away. Charities contacted by one of my mother's friends, a junk dealer Frank knew, a red skip with 'James Murphy & Co.' written in yellow letters on the side. I moved through the house a final time, shoes clattering on stone floors, dull echoes bouncing off bleak walls. It was not the house that held me, embryonic youth. Empty. Spirits flown. I could leave then. I took the photograph in the silver frame. Black and white.

*Dublin. The sound of the name, the images it conjures up. I have not been back in so long now, why does it hold this fascination for me? What powers do its littered streets and drunken buildings hold over me? I gave it up. My choice. And yet . . . A fleeting moment at Heathrow. A rental car, the courtesy coach, a Dublin accent. A fragment of a conversation. Eavesdropper. I can smell the Liffey. I can see the crazed pedestrians risking life and limb to cross O'Connell Bridge. I can taste the Guinness. No other city sounds like this. 'Herald or Press.' The traffic, the people. It was me who chose to cast it from me. I cannot go back. I tell myself that it would not have me back. It was me who cut it from me like a cancer. Me who banished this thing I love as I banish all things that love me. And now it has become my incubus, never to be exorcised.*

*I am a coward. I know that now. I have spent my whole life running. She told me before I lost her. 'Michael, I love you. Christ knows you've never made it easy for me, but I do. It isn't possible for me not to love you. You might as well stop trying to make me hate you. You just want to be able to blame me. You're a coward, Michael. Have the courage to face that. You're a coward.' She was right. I couldn't accept her love because, in recognising it, I would have had to see the inadequacy of what I offered in return. It was easier to blame her. True to form, Michael Dwyer took the path of least resistance.*

A door opens, a door closes. She looks at me. No great warmth, but she is resigned to it now. The hostility has vanished too.

'What do you want, Michael?'

'I don't know. To talk maybe.'

'Come in then.'

This could have been so much different. Sarah asleep on a blanket by the fire, Maria radiant in blue jeans, her blond hair falling loosely around her shoulders. I want to touch her but that is no longer an option for me. She settles a tray on the coffee table. Her face is a mask, intent on what she is doing. I do not exist. I will not exist until she is ready. She pours a cup of tea for me. Slow, precise. The cup and saucer pass from her hands to mine. *Take this cup and drink from it.* She turns back to the table without meeting my eye. She has not looked at me since I arrived. I cannot take my eyes off her.

'Thanks for seeing me.'

Her expression gives nothing away, there is no opening there. She waits. She will not help me.

'I wish things had been different.'

Still nothing.

'Come back with me.'

At this she laughs. 'You poor daft eejit. What do you think this is? The movies? And they all lived happily ever after? Ah, Michael.'

'I meant what I said to you at the graveyard. I do love you. Please come home.'

'I am home, Michael. Like I told you, you can visit Sarah any time you want. In time, we might even be friends. That's as far as it goes. You aren't the one for me. I wish to Christ I'd known that earlier.'

The baby stirs. The fire crackles. The tea scalds my lips. My eyes fill with tears. I tell myself it's the tea. *You blind thick-shit, Dwyer.*

Maria bends over the table and helps herself to two lumps of sugar, her spoon rattling against the side of her cup, her hair spilling across her face. Sarah's eyes are open. She looks up at me and smiles. I want to hold her, but I am afraid. There is a fragile bond between us. I sit there, holding my cup and saucer, the fire warming my cheek, and look into the eyes of my daughter. Everything I want is in this room.

And then it hits me. It really is over. No happy endings for Michael. You've made your bed, so lie in it. Strange business. I always thought that all I had to do was give it time. *It'll all work out in the long run.* I'll never tell you that, Sarah. It simply isn't true. Father Christmas does not exist, there is no such thing as the tooth fairy, there are no monsters in the wardrobe, and nothing ever works itself out. Fuck. I am the worst kind of pilgrim. The promised land has vanished into thin air, the breadcrumbs have been blown away. I cannot go back. Listen to your father, Sarah. I know. I have learned. Listen to me. I have sinned. *And for your penance.* Listen to your father. *Our Father.* Too late. Oh Christ. Listen.

'I had to ask, Maria,' I say softly, almost to myself. 'You know that, don't you?'

'I know, Michael. But it's best like this. You know that too.'

'Yeah. I suppose . . .' Now that I am ready to choose, I find that she has chosen for me. It is what she is used to, being the grown up. 'I should have . . .' No. Too late. 'Don't judge me too harshly, will you, Maria?'

'No. No, of course not. It's strange. I almost understand. I really hope you find what you're looking for, Michael.'

'Yeah.' I smile. 'Me too.' There is nothing else to say.

She sees me to the door and leans over to kiss my cheek.

'Look after yourself, won't you, Michael?'

'I suppose I'll have to now.'

She smiles. Affectionate. Touches my hand. Then she is gone. I climb into the taxi.

'Take me to the airport please.'

'Where are you off to?'

'I wish I knew.'